Teran Tales

Before & After the Machine

by TS Caladan

Teran Tales
Before & After the Machine

Contents

All people, places & events
in the following story are
from a parallel (Earth)
planet called 'Tera.' But
everything is not the same.

Chapter 1:

Before the Great War

The Lizards launched the 'Great War' on Tera in 1935. With the failure of the 'Conference of Nations' in 1929, the planet was primed for a kind of war it had never experienced before: *A World War!*

Britain [Lizard Directors and Generals] *crashed* the American Stock Exchange that same year, which affected the whole planet, just to set the stage for *confusion* and the Great War they had planned for many years. To go back in time:

Before the formation of America and other countries from British Imperial Rule, there had only been small-scale, civil conflicts. Tiny Revolutions. Teran countries did not make war with other Teran countries. The Pre-Industrial Age was primitive, yet people were peaceful, for the most part. Before modern times, natives in most countries lived their lives as various types of Indians. Tribal.

It was a simple time when *trade* for goods and services was as valued as being *paid* for goods and services. People were basically good-natured human beings and helped others in trouble. If young ones lost family, then literally, the 'village' took care of them. Children and the elderly were always respected and were never homeless. Major crimes did not occur in days of long ago. People worked and had a sense of "community" and gave back to the community.

There were no political wars or holy wars. It was left up to individual citizens exactly what they thought / believed, religiously, scientifically, politically or philosophically. There were no organized religions or churches across all the lands of Tera. Such religious beliefs were always held as very private and personal matters, never shared publicly with any type of ceremony.

Young people were carefully educated by family members more so than within organized schools. The first schools were excellent agencies filled with teachers who cared about students and relayed important information about Life and living a good life. As time passed, teachers cared less and less and so did their students. As time went on, families were not as close as they once were in the past. What exactly happened in the prehistoric past was a major mystery to Terans.

Suddenly, the 20th Century arrived and with it came modern machinery and new technologies. This was primarily because of one man, Nikola Tesla, who was a Venusian and was called: "The Man Who Fell to Tera" and "Superman of the Industrial Age." People of Tera never knew the real story of "the *man* who invented the 20th and 21st Centuries," but they were made very familiar with the *Superman Story*. Tesla's real parents landed on Tera in 1856 and gave their infant son to a couple of intelligent, talented and loving Terans who raised him as their own. Tesla did his best to fit into society, but he was always very aware that he was an *alien.* His purpose was to light the way and place humanity on the road to utopia, a high-tech Future, which will happen in the next century.

Radio, television, X-rays, radar, electron microscope, all forms of lighting, which were powered by Tesla's awesome Alternating Current and not Tommie Edison's stupid direct current, were only a few of the early inventions of the wonder-boy. These awesome inventions and principles were from the 19th Century.

Radio changed the world in 1910 with the first radio station, KDKA, in Pittsburgh, PA. This was because Tesla was funded by George Easthouse, a well-known Pittsburgh philanthropist. Music, big bands, orchestras, jazz, were now heard from great distances! The concept of a "magic box" that spoke and played music and gave news, wowed Terans that were still stuck in the old-fashioned Victorian Age. Plays/dramas/ads were broadcast over this new medium. Radio was used onboard the U.S.S. Titanic in 1912 when it struck an iceberg head-on. Radio quickly alerted rescue ships, averted a potentially huge disaster and may have saved hundreds of lives at sea.

Television changed the world, but the masses were not given access to television until decades after it was invented. Television was another suppressed technology, until the Reptiles decided that it should be made available to the general public. The story of TV's creation is an unbelievable story that was kept out of schoolbooks and away from Terans. Nikola Tesla attempted to '**Photograph Thoughts**' with one of his inventions in 1928 *and he succeeded!* According to a few Colorado newspapers like the 'Sentinel.' The mystery was the fact that in the years to come, his "Thought Visualizer" never saw the light of day. It was 'swept under the rug' along with hundreds of other patents that were far too advanced to ever be made real in the 20th Century. Not in an age where Lizards maintained a strict superiority and control over human beings. Water engines, antigravity, weather-control machines, motors powered by collector-dish arrays and other fantastic things were simply suppressed and went into a large Tesla-file of "missing patents." Lizards had no intention of allowing Tesla's super inventions to exist or him laying the groundwork for the World of Tomorrow so soon. Yet, television was allowed and would never have happened unless: Nikola Tesla realized that *thoughts left an impression on the retina.* That impression could be enhanced and broadcast. The same principle was used in the creation of Cathode-ray television.

Nations had built armies and now the new *aeroplanes* greatly added to countries' offensive weaponry. But these militias were utilized as Police Forces within the borders of their respective countries and never attacked neighboring nations, outside of "tiny revolutions." In this way, Tera survived and Terans did not have "war in their veins" or memories or a need for large-scale Wars.

Today was different with the new age of radio, television, quick air travel by jet planes and the possibility of atomics. Tera got smaller and smaller everyday because of the popularity of radio and television. Modern times of global communications created a *Golden Age* for citizens. Society was suddenly aware of the "Global Community" and different ways, methods and beliefs of a wide range of cultures. Television was an amazing tool for LEARNING and that was how it was utilized in its first days right after the Great War.

Everything had seemed glorious at the start of the 20th Century. Then came the New York Stock Market Crash of 1929 where everyone on the planet felt its economic 'sting.' The world was led to believe (by Reptilians, through Britain) that *Fear* crashed the NY Exchange, in the same way as investors in a Bonzi Scheme panicked and wanted their investments back and there was no money to be returned. ***Crash!*** But this was not the true story. The truth was: Britain could have printed more money and saved the day for all of Tera. No. Instead, the situation had been established from the beginning to fail just as it did on that particular day of "Black Friday." There was absolutely nothing to fear, no real reason to panic; share values had always slowly increased and were proven to be generally profitable.

Dips in profits had occurred, while news agencies pumped out false stories that investors had "lost life-savings." Not true, but people never questioned newspapers and reporters in the *good ol' days*. If it was in the newspapers, people believed it. People were paid to lie and they swayed the public away from the truth.

Then the 'seeds' of WAR were planted. The Conference of Nations was a group of leaders from the top 33 countries (economically speaking). The special group was considered the "first world organisation." They had met 13 times in the years between 1930 and 1935 in order to ensure peace for the world *in these uncertain times*. It was the "Promise of Peace" that grabbed the attention of Terans as new tech and weaponry had developed, such as: guided missiles, submarines, guided torpedoes, tanks, fighter jets, aircraft carriers and larger payloads of cannon fire. People of all nations worried, especially with whispers of an Ultimate Bomb that *destroyed cities!* Terans were desperate for "Good News" in times of fear and the Conference of Nations, or C.O.N., gave them hope for a better tomorrow.

Secret Lizard Controllers understood the situation and understood what must happen in the years to come. Terans did not have a clue.

The British General-Secretary held "the note" high for the cameras of the World Press that assured all citizens that "German military forces planned no aggression against any nation." But in 1935, Paris was attacked by the Luftwaffe and their fire-bombs! *Hundreds of Parisians were killed! The city was on fire! The Eiffel Tower was also damaged and remains slightly tilted.*

English Royals [Lizard Directors] orchestrated every bit of conflict that led up to and was "the Great War," "the War to End All Wars." Hegelian Dialectics: "They" controlled both sides, the peaceniks and the warmongers. They planned every aspect of WAR from the U.S. War Room inside the Pentagon. Covert Lizards made sure the largest building on the planet, where they had designed all wars, was in the shape of Witchcraft's Pentagram. Only insiders knew. Outsiders had no idea that the monuments of Washington, D.C. stood at the 5-points of that Pentagram. The Great War had been planned for a very long time...

Why? It was a complex question. 1) On one hand, no large conflicts between countries in the past? The world was ripe for an Armageddon, or *one hell of a conflagration* that came close to THE END. 2) Wasn't an all-out exercise in the new weapons and new (destructive) technologies needed? Didn't the inventors of the rockets and missiles and bombs require a really big test? 3) Reptile Overlords were curious. What would happen? They designed a Story, as fake as any story, that Terans were forced into believing~. Would they? The

Test was a Test of the Human Heart. Would citizens buy a Fake War as a real one? Or will they reject the wave of hatred, fear and war in the air and in the ground and turn toward Peace instead?

The people were forced/pushed through the Media-Machine and believed that "War would be good for the global economy" and will have citizens *working.*

Lizard Royals operated *under the skin* of human royals that sat on the throne of England and a few other monarchies. The concept was: Give the people the bloodiest war, thanks to new advancements in machines (weaponry), and that violence would be so horrific and devastating that "it would never happen again." After bloody battles over a 10-year period, *War* would be "out of Terans' systems" and there would be an age of lasting peace in the future. The Lizards who had always retarded human growth as a species were not against Tesla's inevitable Wireless World of the Future. They viewed the tremendous Tomorrow in their Time Machines, Time Windows and Minority Reports. A glorious New Age of technology laid ahead for the human race. The Lizards stood united against the idea that Teran Utopia should begin in the 20th Century. They believed "people could only handle a small degree of progress at a time." Too many quantum leaps too fast could be disastrous, as ancient (lost) history had proved.

The unknown factor in Teran affairs at the time was

the atom bomb. Why was it really created? The *story* handed to World Press was certainly not the truth (90% = always untrue). Robert Oppenheimer was a joke, a front, like other front-men liars who were given credit for things they did not do. In truth, the Lizards assigned to Tera were also being tested, tested by Higher Authorities in the universe. The Allies' nuclear explosion that vaporized Odo Island as a warning was viewed in various Time Portals. **The horrible devastation of a 3-mile, unpopulated island!** This was the crucial point. Will the atomic detonation immediately end the signs and inception of war? But. What if Tojo and Hitler did not surrender to the Allies after the blast, firestorm and fall-out? What then? Do the Reptiles, through the aristocracy, actually destroy Hong Kong?

The latest news among Lizards, which proved the Reptilian Race was also being played as Puppets, was that *Rogue Lizards had appeared!* They had assumed/acquired the shapes of some of the most powerful people on the planet. The GAME where simple natives were caught in the crossfire, got a lot more complicated. There was a sudden and very real inner *War among Reptiles!* Here was a group of Enemy Lizards to the prime set of Lizards put in charge of Tera. They wanted a whole other scenario to occur in history. They used their Generals and minions of Generals to not push for peace, but to "double-down" and *force an all-out World War!* How could this have happened? Lizard vs.

Lizard in an invisible war within human skins? Unprecedented. Had the universe gone mad in this push for *war, war, war?!* Some Lizards wanted a bright future for Humanity and now there was another (secret) group of Reptiles that pushed for total war and the possibility of destruction of the entire planet? Which group of dark green, scaly Overlords would win?

And because of the new, forced direction...

A huge campaign occurred among Hollywood's glitterati. Celebrities of all countries, not just America, fanned the flames of Hatred and War! Everyone had to do their part for the War to come. People read of atrocities committed by Adolph Hitler and his men on a daily basis. Pre-war shortages happened, when there was really an abundance of supplies. War bonds were purchased by most citizens. Women did their part in a non-combative way and men enlisted for war. More men joined the ranks. More and more and this was the failed test. Americans had the choice to join England's insane war or not to join England's insane war? Most succumbed to the daily propaganda in newspapers, in movies, in photos and on Movie Newsreels. The world marched toward War, closer and closer each day.

Those who resisted enlistment were considered "cowards, sissies and faggots" if you did not Serve Your Country. Those "peaceniks," for the most part, comprised a mere 5% of the general public. Most everyone was enraged more and more with the terrible lies they read in papers and heard on the news. Everything was in place as Tera became a giant powder keg that waited for a match.

After the destruction of Odo Island by the BOMB that did not result in the surrender of Nazi and Chinese forces, the 'Crimson Wave' bombed Pearl Harbor [on another 'Black Tuesday,' December 9th] and the Nazis' "Blitz" bombed the American and British undergrounds.

Now, there was World War. This was exactly what the Lizards had planned, only they themselves were being tested and were unaware they were also 'under the microscope.'

Chapter 2:

War to End All Wars

For the last 5 years, there were two *fronts* pushed heavily by the early Media and that was: 1) Horrible stories of Hitler's gay, perverted, Nazi generals and other minions that ordered fire-bombings, first-strikes against innocent citizens and carried out tortures and unspeakable things as scientific experiments! 2) Every able-bodied citizen should enlist and join the fight against a fascist takeover of the planet!

Hitler's Germany and Communist Red China had joined forces: their armies, their technologies and their air forces, 'the Crimson Wave' and 'the Iron Fist.' The leaders of these countries were portrayed as *monsters*. German tanks and planes invaded Poland, Switzerland, the Czech Republic, Russia, Italy, other targets and maintained a base in France. Chinese forces under the command of Emperor Tojo bombed islands and areas around the Pacific. China and Germany utilized highly-armed U-boats and submarines and brought great destruction to military and passenger vessels on both oceans.

Japan remained neutral during the War. They became isolationists because of their resemblance to Chinese people, especially to Westerners. Japanese islands became safe havens for all Asian ['Orientals' back then] people. Asians located in many countries migrated to Japan during the Great War. There was a secret treaty between China and Japan that was unknown by Teran outsiders: *China would never bomb Japanese-owned islands,* but they would attack islands that did not belong to Japan. Japan was never attacked.

America was now firmly engaged in England's War. A few small liners attempted crossings between the U.S. and Europe while under military escort. But technical advances in German U-boats caused a large number of casualties. Celebrities like Buster Keaton, Mary Astor, Will Rodgers and Molly Brown were "killed when their ships were sunk by U-boats." Their fake deaths and other known figures (lies) were used as propaganda so more red-blooded boys enlisted, shaved their heads and picked up guns.

The Armed Forces discovered there were too many

young lads willing to go to their deaths for this new cause, this wave, this Movement of Hatred and War! Brother vs Brother. Recruiting stations worldwide were flooded with volunteers who were enraged into mental *furies and frenzies* and could not wait to kill "Krauts." WAR was a completely new experience in Teran history and, today, there were millions of excited youths who were ready to *fight, fight, fight!*

Political cartoons on a daily basis harshly ridiculed and poked fun at both leaders of China and Germany. In-between movies, animated shorts like 'Sad Sack,' 'Betty Toot' and 'Snafu,' urged citizens to do their part. People should conserve on certain foods/materials and to expect shortages on a lot of items in the next few years.

Once again, there were food-lines for bread and milk, etc., just like how it was right after the Stock Market Crash of '29. People in fear hoarded various foods, drinks and materials. In both instances, there were hidden surpluses. But not for the poor people.

The Allies organized under [Warlock and Grand Dragon] Winston Churchill, who called in his masonic forces under him: Russia, America, France, Italy, India, Spain and other militias that were willing to fight against what was called in the newspapers: 'Hitler's Second Reich.'

Those were the battle lines or *teams* onstage for the

Great War. The 'Theatre of War' took a very strange turn when Nikola Tesla was brought in to help eliminate all those nasty sinkings by German U-boats in the Atlantic Ocean. Tesla's solution was simple: **If Allied ships were invisible** to enemy radar, they wouldn't be sunk and would have the advantage with first-strike capabilities. The only problem was ELECTRIC POWER. An intense, mega-amount of Energy was needed to render an aircraft carrier or destroyer *invisible.* People from the 1940s would have to handle such awesome levels of Quantum-Hertz, EM Power that...

A lot could go wrong!! And on the very first test, at the Naval shipyard of Philadelphia Bay, <u>something went drastically wrong</u>! Before this, Nikola Tesla walked off the big, secret project. He was upset that the government (Britain) would not spend the extra dollars for Zero-Point wristbands for everyone onboard the test vessel (Destroyer-class) called the U.S.S. Cleaver. The bands would have "grounded" the soldiers and technical experts on the destroyer. Each person could never have been "unstuck in time and space," no matter what occurred to the ship. Other heated arguments ensued and Tesla quit. Navy officials were sure with the help of Albert Einstein, Niels Bore, Townsend Brown and Al Bielek, they could complete Tesla's Project without his final calculations. They were very wrong. On May 1, 1941, Al Beliek and his brother threw the *third switch* onboard the Cleaver and something massively unexpected happened...

The Destroyer-class vessel of 10,000 tons VANISHED!

No one thought along the lines of the alien from Venus. His solution to *cloaking* ships was not magically having U.S. ships disappear from radar screens of enemy ships...it was to *literally have the Navy vessels really DISAPPEAR* or beam to another location, which is what happened with the U.S.S. Cleaver! When the third lever was pulled that ratcheted up the Power to Maximum, a **Black Hole Vortex** was created in front of the ship's bow! (pictured) It sucked in everything around it that even included the heavy mist on that fateful Tuesday morning.

TV cameras recorded and caught everything on film: The mini-Black Hole got larger and larger and expanded to a point where it *swallowed the destroyer!* Whole! And after loud buzzes and a bright, electrical lightshow over the entire ship, *there was no more Cleaver in Philadelphia Bay!!* Gone. The event surprised Einstein, Bore and Brown, and other observers who remained on the mainland. Al Bielek and his brother Duncan witnessed ALL HELL that broke loose onboard the ship! There was no *clean-beam* to another location; the ship was caught in a dimension between time and space. Some soldiers and technicians were fused to bulkheads, some disappeared and were *shifted to other places!* Al and Duncan could not change the 3 locked levers in the Control Room so they decided, through all the chaos of a highly-electrified ship, *to jump ship!* They did. But instead of landing in the waters of Philadelphia Bay where they'd swim to shore, they **bounced to the far future!** The story of Al Bielek and brother Duncan is an incredible story and was portrayed in a Hollywood film that was close to reality. The film left out the 'bounce into the far future.'

'The Philadelphia Experiment,' as the event was known in later years, was actually a battle between the unseen Lizards and their enemy, the unseen Rogue Lizards. Two UFOs in the area were also caught by cameras that recorded the U.S.S. Cleaver. Little did anyone know that positive and negative Reptiles were behind the Experiment (and the Atom Bomb). It was a test. Could Tesla possibly succeed and change History? If he had stayed with the Project and used his final calculations, the ship would have *beamed* without a hitch. This could have ended the war in 7 years without usage of a nuclear bomb. But Time Portals (which were never wrong) showed that the *Great War would last for 10 years and would include a nuked Hong Kong~*. Problems Tesla encountered with the Project came from the U.S. Joint Chiefs of Staff under FDR. At the time, Tesla could not smell *Reptiles,* later he could unmask their disguises. Under Human Skin, a few Rogue Lizards made cases against the Zero-point bands. That ploy sunk the whole Project and extended the War for 3 more years, which was what was supposed to happen.

The survivors of the Philadelphia Experiment were brought to the government facility at Montauk, NY, and they were known as the "Montauk Boys." They were studied by doctors after the event in the same way far future doctors studied Al and Duncan. The radiation and electric/magnetic damage to their bodies was severe, but easily cured in the Wonderworld of Tomorrow with perfect Machines. At primitive Montauk, little could be done for the boys. Some disappeared and reappeared at different places. Some disappeared and never returned. A few seemed to view horrors that others couldn't see. They were not grounded to our timeframe, our place in space and time. They eventually died soon after, while Al and Duncan lived long lives.

Al Bielek and Duncan learned of a fantastic future

under the perfection of "Dream-Maker Machines." +Lizards brought them back: The Great Experiment CRACKED reality, because of the incredible amount of electrical energy that was produced. Exactly like the film showed, a 40-year Wave [electric/magnetic disturbance] affected events 40 years later on 5/1/1981! *Good* Lizards corrected both potentially lethal disasters that would have decimated the planet. How?

They sent Al Bielek and his brother back in time where they were again surrounded by the very hot and getting hotter, electrical generators onboard the U.S.S. Cleaver. This time, there were sledgehammers in the Control Room and they knew to destroy the generators. When they smashed the mechanism...

Reality completely changed! *(to their point of view)* Similar to special-effects seen in movies. This happened. The same linked disaster in two time periods was diverted by (compassionate?) Lizards. Tera's reality changed back into an Uncracked State, because the Black Hole never engulfed the destroyer - the power was cut-off before that happened. Al and Duncan's story is fantastic and absolutely true. One of the greatest human stories, outside of Nikola Tesla's story. The brothers met various aliens, went through time vortexes, worked with Tesla, witnessed the Reptiles, *materialized thoughts* and were beamed from one location to another! Duncan is still alive, but only because after his amazing experiences, *the +Lizards de-aged him* as a "thank you."

He had become one-third of his normal age. He now lives a good life in seclusion as a senior citizen.

'The Gibraltar Experiment' paralleled the Philadelphia Experiment only no outsider knew about it and no one got hurt. No part of the "wild and crazy" story was ever leaked into the public domain. It was actually "small potatoes." Here was one of the few federal secrets that was sealed and 100% covered up...

A year before the event in Philadelphia Bay, one of Nikola Tesla's machines was put to a test. The cannon-like device appeared similar to an Ozone Collector, black, no more than 7-feet high, and its patent read: "Ultraviolet/Infrared Viewer." It was one of very few of his mega-inventions that a typical electrical engineer could build and not have the requirement of a super-genius. Simple to construct. But who knew what would happen after the build-up of energy occurred and the ON switch was depressed?

Previously, British Commanders in charge of their War, refused Tesla's 'Death Ray' Beam Machine! *Refused?* A **Particle-Beam Weapon** could drill a hole through a mountain from 100 miles away! Its rays could make 'Swiss cheese' out of the Moon! And a very/very big one might blot out the Sun!! Why did the British Royals, the most powerful forces on the planet, the evil Money-Printers who control the world...why did they say NO to, at the time, what was the ultimate weapon? The old Council of Nine voted 5-4 against the development of Particle Beam Weapons for any Teran nation. That was only because 5 of the royals were the Old School Lizards, while 4 of them were the young-gun Rogue Reptiles who only secured 4 humans on the Council. *It was that close to have Ultimate Guns in the hands of insane "people."*

The UVIR Viewer was a patent out of the "missing patents" bin, which was deemed either too controversial or too much ahead of its time to ever be constructed. Yet, a "viewer" seemed "safe" and was approved to be covertly built. Possibly there were military or industrial uses for the UVIR Viewer. In a short time, a working model was built and had to be tested.

The Columbian Illuminati again used their infamous date of May First (1940) to conduct the test. Location? The place had to be remote or very isolated. A military presence would be perfect. The island of Gibraltar was a logical choice because it was 'armed to the teeth' with sophisticated weaponry set in place by British Generals and officials from Malta. The island was one of the largest single rocks on Tera and stood directly within the mouth of the Mediterranean. No German U-boat could pass by "the Rock" and attack Allied countries like Italy, Greece, Egypt and the Holy Land. There is an old saying that the "monkeys of Gibraltar will only leave the island when the British do." The tongue-in-cheek message meant: The British will never leave the island, primarily because of its crucial location.

Tesla's "Viewer" surprised everyone who was there and observed the extraordinary and very restricted "phenomenon," "reality-shift," "displacement," "projector," "hallucinator," "mind-fuck Monday..." Those were some of the descriptions that happened that weird day. A total of 88 scientists and military men were in attendance.

Observers, technicians and military personnel expected a Projector, a Viewer, as if the tubular cannon would project a wide movie screen. The principle was: When Ultraviolet and Infrared rays were combined in just the right harmonic frequencies, they acted as a Mind-Viewer to the next parallel universe, the closest one (in frequency) to the frequency of this particular Tera. But, the mechanism did not project a viewing screen, it changed or *tuned reality* in the minds of the observers. The sky was suddenly different, hills in the distance were different and *the land in the foreground! They all observed the new environment!*

THE PEOPLE WERE INSIDE THE OTHER CLOSE PARALLEL WORLD! They did not see it at a distance as one would when a movie was viewed in a theater. *They were there!* In that next world, and were somewhat scared. What they observed was more than extraordinary<>.

Gibraltar was no longer an island. It was a very high point on the Spanish mainland! In fact, the gigantic rock appeared out-of-place with the terrain around it. As if it did not fit with the topography, yet there it was...in a different position, not an island. Cannons, big-gun placements, hidden enclosures for machine guns and also the airstrip that was on the island of Gibraltar...was no longer on an island in the waters of the Gibraltar Straits, *but was upon a very high Rock attached to the flat, Spanish mainland!* The monkeys were still on the Rock.

Technicians struck the OFF switch after 3 minutes and 37 seconds and *BANG!* Instantly what seemed real to the senses, a similar but different Tera, was switched *off.* The device powered-down. The island of Gibraltar that the scientists and military officials were familiar with, returned. The main man at the Switch was going to immediately hit the *switch* when they realized the device was not a Projector and messed with their minds, but he was waved off by a higher General. The top General [Lizard] was curious and wanted the 'mind-menagerie" to last a little longer...

After 3 and a half minutes, the observers got bored and ended the show. The device went back into the Missing Patents Bin and was never used again. Nobody appeared hurt or affected at all. The medical tests were 'negative' and there were no ill after-effects. It was as if the observers simply went inside a movie that had a slightly different setting. The UVIR Viewer was deemed "useless" and certainly had no military applications. A few papers were written on and about the Gibraltar

Experiment and the whole affair was marked 'classified.' What did two worlds mean? Possibly future minds might answer the question?

The Great War went on and on and the common people were about sick of it, but had no power to stop it. More territories were taken by the Nazis. More invasions into Balkan countries and Scandinavian countries. The Germans fought on too many fronts. More casualties in horrific air battles and fights at sea. Nothing made sense. Battle tactics were purposely designed so that soldiers died rather than sound tactics where there were military victories. This was because Madness ruled, no one would win and the killing simply went on and on. Why? Because all parties in the War took orders from Britain, the secret architects. There were attempts to kill Hitler and everyone of them had failed. The 'Valkyrie' bombing had injured Hitler, but did not kill him. At one point the world celebrated his death! Only to find that it was the murder of his brother-in-law double, the Fuhrer's chauffeur. Millions of people had been killed as a result of the Great War. After nearly 10 years, no one thought it was "great." Terans wanted peace and they wanted it very soon. So did the +Lizards. The -Lizards wanted the War to last indefinitely, 10 or 20 more years, at least, as if humanity could survive under such hellish conditions? People had no idea that there were wars within wars and more wars within wars.

There was too much carnage, too much human damage, too much pain for the +Lizards to bear. They wanted a quick end to the World War, like Tesla wanted, which defied all Laws of Physics: **the Future was fixed** and could not be changed. The Great War was supposed to last for ten years and for no more. The future was oddly cloudy and vague when it came to the Atom Bomb. Was the nuke going to be used on the Chinese or not? The fear was: With this new element of *Rogue Mad Reptiles,* the War might continue forever? That future was never seen. But now that a great many factors in reality have changed? Who knew the real truth or what would wind up as reality? Could Tesla's Wireless World of Tomorrow NEVER happen for Terans, not in any century? These *changes* were the new concerns for the positive Overlords who had managed the War and were blinded about Tomorrow.

The Big Question was: Will Hong Kong need to be nuked as a means to end the War? Events were never supposed to get that far. The "Odo Island Event" of a small mushroom cloud and the island's awesome disintegration failed. The Atom Bomb was never to be really used on the Chinese people; it was the <u>threat</u> of oblivion that was supposed to bring a lasting Peace and peace treaties among nations. But with negative Lizards on the Council of 12 and new, unexpected battles at hand...anything and everything could change with a future in flux~.

The -Lizards compromised and sanctioned the use of the atomic bomb. These dark events (the destruction of Hong Kong) WILL END THE 10-YEAR LONG WORLD WAR! Good Lizards believed the war would run its course, people would be tired of sending their sons to death, and the Great War would terminate on its own. Without a nuclear explosion! There was no Big Bomb detonation upon Hong Kong seen in Time Windows. The good Lizards also realized that there never would have been an atomic bomb if not for the dark *Influence* of Rogue Lizards, a group that was not foreseen in any Time Portal.

The sad vote for the positive Lizards was a compromise: There would be no lasting War that continued decade after decade. The Great War would end, which saddened the negative Lizards who wanted it to go on. But the War would only end after the horrors of a nuclear detonation were displayed for the world><. *Millions of innocent Chinese people would be burned, crushed, killed by a single Bomb so that a lasting peace and a better tomorrow will be the final result.* That was the hope, anyway...

Lizard Engineers of the War made sure that the plane that dropped the Atom Bomb on Hong Kong would have a coded designation which connected with their unholy '666.' 'B' (2) plus 'F' (6) = 8 and add '7,4,8' (19) = **27**. 27 is 3 9s.

The Great War ended on December 7, 1945! It finally ended. Newspapers declared: PEACE! And the world rejoiced in happiness! The Columbian Illuminati was not happy. Corporations that pumped out weaponry were not happy. Winston Churchill was not happy. Tojo and Adolph Hitler were not happy and many royal minions were not pleased at all. Everyone else was *thrilled, delighted and celebrated a peace-time the public had not known for a decade!* "A Day that will live in the hearts of men and will mean freedom for all people." Those were Franklin Delano Rosevelt's famous words after the end of the Great War...that Churchill's men told the minion to say.

Chapter 3:

Steve Jurci

A small story inside the larger story of the Great War concerned one of its participants, Steven Raymond Jurci. It was December 7, 1945. He had just heard his man, the President of these good ol' United States of America, who announced the END OF THE WAR! Hitler and Tojo were defeated and surrendered after the Bomb was dropped. It was really, finally, actually over. Too many good people had died during ten years of hell! For what? It did not matter now because today there was peace<. Everyone felt it. Bells of Freedom rang in all corners of Tera! The planet will party now; it was time for glorious celebrations, festivals and good times. It was a time to be with your families and also to *make babies!* Women greeted their brave men as they returned home. People couldn't be happier! Tomorrow's headlines read: "**WAR ENDS!**" And other variations of what had occurred in China. It was in this bright, hopeful atmosphere where people can love and go back to being human beings and not automatic machines, that...

TS Caladan

Steven Jurci strangely passed on attending a number of parties and private parties thrown by his Navy buddies. He decided to be anti-social. He'd have a quiet night, alone, in a hotel room and make his way back home to Bridgeville, Pennsylvania the very next day. But. Unforeseen things sometimes happen that change everything in the world. The young man 'hit the hay' early in the evening so he could make a day of it with a happy homecoming. He had a big family and there was a certain lady who gave him her picture, Rose. It's been three years, but he knew she'd still be waiting for him. Tomorrow looked fantastic!

Steve made it out of the War with his arms, legs and head intact. He had a few close calls being in the Navy. There was the time when a Chinese Crimson Wave plane crashed on the deck of his destroyer! Huge explosion! A few crewmen instantly died. Steve was in the lower decks when the plane crashed. If not for *"Marconi's"* Wireless onboard to S.O.S. another Allied vessel in the area, his whole crew would have had it. He saved a small piece of the Chinese plane and kept it as a souvenir. *My future-son might like it,* he thought. Steve remembered another time when his hero, FDR, gave an amplified speech to many of the Commander-in-Chief's ships out on Honolulu Bay. A malfunction happened and a torpedo was discharged from his destroyer and *exploded* when it struck shore! The blast was about 300 feet from where the President spoke at the podium. A general alarm rang out and Steve remembered that *all the gun turrets of more than 40 large vessels were pointed at his destroyer!* Could an enemy have gained access to the ship and launched a torpedo at the President? No. It was a true malfunction, an accident, but Steve thought it would be ironic "to be shot down by your own ships." Those were the only incidents where young Steve thought he might die after 3 years in the service. But the War was behind him now. He daydreamed of a better tomorrow and it would really happen now. He couldn't wait to get home and for the calm light of a New Day. Peacetime. A very needed peace everyone deserved. Maybe that's why he tried to sleep earlier than normal? Hurry tomorrow, and reach home. The odd twist in the story is...

In that *twilight* between Light and Dark or sleep and non-sleep, Steve had a *'One Step Beyond'* experience that he did not expect. He suddenly felt a presence in his hotel room [#101]. The young man in a crew cut sat up and was now wide awake. He knew or *felt* he wasn't alone. He did not hear anything when he said, "Who's there? ...I said who's there? I know yer there..." The young man jumped to his feet and felt *fear*. "Something's going on. With my luck, war's over and cold Death's at my door 'cos I died of Happiness the night before. Huh." A chill ran up the Navy man's spine and he felt something brush by him. "Aah."

"I didn't mean to bump you, da...I mean, please don't freak out. Not freak out. You can hear my voice. Yes, there, Navy-guy? Hear me? Don't be scared. YER DREAMIN' yeah, that's all...and I'm, I'm a ghost. But I'm a friendly ghost, like Casper. You know Casper, the friendly ghost? Yes?"

Steve was angry. "What the hell do you want?! No, no!....(pause)...you, ah, y-you still there, Casper? Maybe that new tooth is pickin' up somethin' in the air like radio? I 'eard of that. I wonder...?" The man walked around, grabbed his pants, shirt and shoes. He put them on. [No voice]. "...So I *was* hearin' things? Hey, buddy. This is not a dream." Steve was shaken. He didn't believe in angels or if there were angels, "Why would they speak to me?" He shook his head. He stretched and then said: "Maybe I *could* use a drink? Huh. Anyway, thank God yer gone there, Casper..." Steve smiled.

The Voice clearly expressed the words: *"No, man. I'm still here."*

"Aaah!" Mister Jurci, shipman 3rd Class, bolted out of the door as fast as a bullet! He screamed as he ran down the hallway! Steve had to have a change of atmosphere, to sort out what had just happened. He came to the conclusion that the room was *haunted. That's the ticket. That's all it was. Like a haunted house, a haunted room. Ha. Casper, 'e said. Maybe it was a friendly ghost* were thoughts that buzzed inside the seaman's head.

Steve walked down the main street of port-town, East McKeesport. Earlier in the day, he saw that a bar was there. A light rain fell, which did not stop groups of people and couples who celebrated the end of the war. Music, joyous shouts were heard. There were a lot of happy drunk people on the streets of East McKeesport and in the world.

The sailor, or former sailor, entered the Blue Salamander, which was an establishment that had told their patrons they would close in a half hour (to be home with family, some returned). Many customers decided to take their festivities to other parties and other saloons. Few people remained. Steve took a few Pabst Blue Ribbon beers to a booth in the corner that was away from others who sat at the bar. He smiled, raised a glass and nodded when a loving couple smiled and raised their glasses at him.

It was perfect. He drank, relaxed. He wouldn't be bothered for a while. Steve wasn't sure how long he'd stay in that room? He planned to throw only the essentials in his bag and run out of there as fast as he could. He drank more, burped. A few more people left. He sighed. He closed his eyes, thought of his girl and smiled a big smile.

Then, in the air around him, he heard, *"I thought you were a tough-guy, old man? Running from a ghost like a little baby? I'm shocked..."*

Steve jumped to his feet and nearly spilled the beers. "It's not the room, it's *me* who's haunted?" He was ready to run again<.

"Stop, stop. You can't get way from me. Let me introduce myself. I'm yer son..."

"My son?!" Steve shouted loud and the couple heard him. He waved it off and they waved back at him. From then on, Jurci changed. He was curious, eased into the booth seat and treated the Voice like he was a seated person. He repeated at a lower register, "My son?"

"Yeah, look. I even say 'yer' for 'you are,' just like you do. You passed along a lot of things to me, like stubbornness and pig-headedness."

"Wait. Casper? I've always said: if I ever had a son, I'd name him...ah, what's yer name, boy?"

"Boy? Who you callin' 'boy,' boy? My name is Doug and I'm 72 years old."

"Ha, ha, ha! Seventy-two!? Wait, fuck, did you say yer name's 'Doug'?"

"Yeah, dad. You named me after Douglas Fairbanks. Your hero. You saw 'The Thief of Bagdad' when you were a kid. It was your Star Wars at the time, you never saw anything like it where you dreamed that you were the prince in the end with the treasure, the cloak of Invisibility, the Girl and flew on a Flying Carpet over fantastic, Arabian architecture....right, dad?"

Steve, uncharacteristically, *cried* because the Voice just proved that it was his son from the future.

"Well, I lived to see the day, daddy. I should hit you in the head for crying. That's an inside joke you won't get."

"Doug? And, and, and...yer mother? Her...n-name?"

"Rose was the only one for you, dad. You know that."

Stevie cried more and drank more. "Rose and I really got married? I really had a son?"

"Well, ha, about that. It's very complicated. I have a confession...Stevie. I'm not, not exactly your son, Okay?"

"Ulp. What the hell? Now yer *not* my son?"

"You almost did a spit-take...It's difficult to explain. Man, I wish you did some serious mind-drugs, but they didn't exist in this black and white time period and all you have is BOOZE! Drink away, dad. Here goes. I'm sure you've never heard of parallel worlds? Right?"

"What are parallel worlds?"

"There is not one universe; there are infinite universes..."

"Why would there be infinite universes? One isn't good enough?"

Doug's spirit expressed, *"Ha, ha. Just believe me, Okay? The ghost knows. Ever stand between two mirrors?"*

"Yeah, at a carnival. You mean all the reflections you see? Those are other universes?"

"No, dad, and let me call you dad for now, alright? The endless reflections in-between two mirrors symbolize parallel worlds that go on forever, only some are drastically different from one another and some are only a little different from one another. Understand?"

A curious and confused Steve said, "Go on..."

"Alright. Hope you can grok, I mean, understand what I'm going to say next. Here goes. My name is Doug, but not Doug Jurci. In most respects, we are father and son, the same blood in our veins, the same good crop of hair, ha, but..."

"But?"

"In my world, yer daddy, my grandpap, changed his name to Y..U..R..C..H..E..Y."

"Why would he change our last name?"

"Because Americans kept mispronouncing how it was said in Czechoslovakia. They kept saying the 'J,' which was silent, of course. So he legally changed it to how it was phonetically pronounced."

"Shucksy Loopy. He was a proud man. And you? You were stuck with a yucky name?"

"I changed it to a cool name when I became an author..."

"You write books? Son, I'm so proud, but wait *yer not my son,* you said. I'm..."

"It's confusing and complicated, young guy. Maybe this is a dream-wish and I'm long dead, who knows? Fulfilling a last request? I wanted to talk to my dad during the war. It was a wish that I could tell him so much. Now, I'm invisible, walkin' around with you in 1945. Yer the closest thing to dad around here so you'll have to do. You see, where I come from and when I come from, much is the same and much is different. My planet isn't called Tera, it's called Earth..."

"Earth?" Steve replied with surprise. He nearly finished his second Blue Ribbon beer. Steve interrupted the Voice and said: "Hey, maybe *I'm* dead? Ha. That would be funny, eh? And this is *my* dream-wish, that, that I could talk to my son from the future when he was all grown up and, and he could tell me about his world?" Steve's face lit up, happy, excited by the thought.

The son said in a sad tone: *"Yeah, sure."* Then he perked up and said: *"You told me once that right after the war, you took ma to a war-film in the theater and when planes came on the screen, you fell on the floor of the theater, ha. I can believe that involuntary reaction, dad."*

"Oh, look. They're waving to us. I guess we should leave now?" Stevie got to his feet.

"Right," Doug said. *"Let's take a walk. I'll follow you."*

Outside, the streets were wet and it was cold, but the man and the Voice did not feel the cold air. They passed shops, cars and happy people that had one beautiful thing in common: The Great War was over. Steve walked to a park that was not too far away. After minutes went by, he found himself alone (sort of) on a park bench and in the dark.

"Yer cars are wild, dad. If I can still call you dad?"

"That sounds good to me too. Hopeful. And I can call you 'son'...ah, ha, even though yer from...*another planet?*"

"It's almost the same as your Tera, like a mirror-image with some differences. I'm sure we'll be talking about the differences. But I don't know if that's the purpose of our meeting like this? It could be about me unloading what I know about the war? You'll never believe me, father. Never. I hope that you can. I don't want to argue or fight with you, old man. We've done that enough as I grew up..."

"Wait. I was a bad father?"

"No. You were a fine father. The Steve I knew cared very much about his wife and only son. You did the best you could. Only, only you were a very stubborn man..."

"You said that before..."

"I'd never lie to you, father. You taught me honesty. But...but..."

"But what?" Steve asked the empty darkness around him.

"I know a lot about the world. I know how it basically works; I've made a study of it. We have computers in the future. It's like a super-huge 'Book of Knowledge' right there at your fingertips. I hold much more true knowledge in my big head than in your little, ignorant head. Sorry to say that. I'm also sorry to say that what I have to tell you will only upset you and piss you off. Then what? The last thing I want to do is fight with you, again, argue about a politician or a concept that you just can't get into your thick head. Dad. Compared to me and what I know at 72 years old...you are a little child in yer crib, young man."

"What if I promise not to get mad? You've warned me to

expect the unexpected. Now I know, and I'll, I'll brace myself. I *am* an honest guy. I'll believe you, son. How bad could the truth be, I mean?"

"Ha, ha, ha. Very mature of you. I hear ya now and we'll see if I believe you later."

"Shoot. I can take it."

"There's so much more beyond the fact that Football is Fixed..."

"What did you say?" Jurci was caught completely off-guard.

"Ha, this is deja vu to me so let's not get into football. Ever hear of a boxer named Rocky Marciano?"

"Yeah, he's that young turk that's been undefeated climbin' up the ranks."

"Yeah, he will become the only undefeated heavyweight champion and become your idol. You'll love the movie they made of his life. Thing is...his boxing matches were rigged, dad."

"They were, or are?"

"He's Italian, just like mom. Put the two and two together, eh?"

"Hold on, now. Hold on, now. You said your world was not the same as mine. Well, doesn't that mean that everything you'll tell me, is, is..."

"Yes, suspect, and should be questioned. Very perceptive, kid. The planet, everything, it's close enough, with bizarre differences. For example, my Allied Forces during the Great War didn't fight against Germany and China...they fought against Germany and Japan..."

"Japan? We have no issue with Japan. Although, many were placed in Internment Camps during the war, because..."

"Say it, father. Because of a resemblance to those damn Chinese people, right?! And what was the issue with the Chinese?"

"Hey! I know a little about what's going on in my time and not your time, Sonny. Those damn Orientals sided with Hitler! The Chinese people sided with the Fuhrer's takeover."

"No, they didn't. Chinese leaders like Tojo were forced to side with Hitler and the people were forced to follow along because of BRITAIN. It's like a machine. No one can go against Freemasonic Royal Orders. Question: Was it fair that Japanese people, good Japanese Americans in this country that called themselves 'Americans,' women and children, were imprisoned and all their possessions confiscated?"

Steve only thought to answer: "We didn't know who were spies and who were not."

"Exactly, so you rounded them all up before they could get to safety in Japan?"

"...Yes."

"Was that fair to innocent Japanese people?"

"No."

"Oh, so you know what fairness is, Stevie?"

The sailor was on the verge of tears again. "Yes."

"Let me tell you good news: The father I knew was a very fair man. He was the bravest and most honest man I've ever known."

Steve cried.

Doug continued: *"I'm brave too, in a different way. You taught me to stick to my guns. If yer right, go out and prove it. But we were as different as night and day. Look at your hair..."*

"What do you mean?"

"Long hair means Freedom, short hair means Slavery. In my youth, my hair was on my shoulders, just like other boys of my era. Look at old paintings and photos. Manly men had long hair and not just because there weren't barber shops. Think about what you remember or seen from before the war. Normal hair was medium or long. It was the fucking Great War that made everyone the same unit, cog, unthinking clone. All the soldiers had to be buzz-cut? No they didn't. They didn't in that little Revolutionary War from way back, right? England doesn't want dissension, defiance, difference! They want uniformity. You can't object, you can only obey."

"I never looked at it that way before."

"Oh, also, we smoked a lot of marijuana..."

"What?! They just busted Robert Mitchem the other day! You smoked that shit?!?"

"Ah! I smoke good shit on a daily basis, dad, or I did when I was alive. There again, you go off talking about something you don't know! Who knows more about pot, you, who have never smoked it and only read horror-stories of Reefer Madness about it in the paper? Or me, who knows that in 2014 hemp, its real and ancient name, became LEGAL. Because it was always a powerful medicine. It's sold in specialty stores like wine and beer. The Indians smoked it in their peace pipes. It makes you relax and yer not stressed out about things, see? It's a God-given resource that has a billion industrial uses. Hey, cowboy! Yer the victim of Weed Propaganda, just like you were the victim of Nazi Propaganda..."

"Look, *Dougie,* which is what I would have called you, yer tellin' me: kids back in your time all had long hair? Down to their shoulders? Ah, whoa. Whoa. What did you just say? How am I, a sailor who just served his country in war, a victim of Kraut propaganda?"

"Okay. First question. I wish people of my time, presently, were long-haired Freedom-Fighters! Times have changed, and changed, and changed again. I guess you'd like the bald youth and skinheads of my time upon appearance, that is. But if you got to know them, the 'Children of the Future' I called them...you would only be thoroughly disgusted. Sickened to your stomach, if given a chance to see my times and my life in the next century. You thought the 21st Century would be fantastic to see, huh? A little like flying over Arabian architecture on a magic carpet with the gold and the girl? Well. Streets are not paved with gold, father. In fact, it's hell...and, and I don't want to show it to you."

"Your times are that bad, son?"

"I don't want you to see my life in 2023, dad. If it was you in my shoes, you'd be screaming! Ha. Oh, and Mother Russia, our friend during the Great War, has been America's or the Free World's New Enemy for almost the last 75 years..."

"What?"

"...England has to set the world ablaze as it always has. The American Super Power needed another Super Power in real games called 'Cold Wars' where a lot of people died and it's always for the same reason, dad: no reason at all. They're just de-populating us 'cos there's too many of us vermin. The insanity to <u>always have war</u> and never have peace!? You think everything was wonderful after 1945? HELL NO! Cold War after Cold War, in the mid-East, Africa or parts of Europe. Meaningless deaths, like a boot

stomping a face, forever. No end."

"In the age of the Atom Bomb? We believed 'Peace-Keeper' would do just that. I guess we were played like fools all along, eh? You said I'm a victim of Nazi Propaganda. Explain how I am a victim of Nazi Propaganda. I don't see that."

*"Again, exactly right. You don't see it. Not German propaganda, **British brainwashing!** 'Nazi' is an English word. 'Nazi' does not mean 'National Socialists.' You used to praise FDR, Churchill's man in the Order. Hey! They take orders from Hitler, who takes orders from...* They *were the ones who destroyed the economy in the first place! They lie to you. England has always lied to us. We remain a colony or one kingdom of the United Kingdom. All countries are still secretly within the British domain. They only gave us those little revolutions where countries have the illusion that they won and were sovereign, but they're not. France, Russia and the United States. England purposely lost the revolts to pump up their colonies worldwide with false freedoms and to secretly control them later on. We are all under the Iron Fist of British Royals who are Nazis. 'Nazi' means to **Not See** something. You are the victim of fascists as long as you Not See what they are doing and what they have done...to all of us. Not the people of England, dad. Monarchies, corporations, control everything. Father. I've actually seen rare photos of the British Royal Family all giving the Nazi salute, even little Elizabeth."*

"Son. The British have been fighting against German Nazis for the last ten years! They're not Nazis."

The Voice in the dark explained: *"I don't know what they are 'under the skin,' but I do know there is evidence that the Throne of England ordered the Luftwaffe to bomb the London underground during the Blitzkrieg. Then, the warplanes that made it to the United States also bombed the safehouses of our undergrounds.*

How'd they know where they were? Why didn't they bomb Parliament or Whitehall or Badmoral Castle? All because rich Money-Printers ordered German air forces to bomb poor people. They don't care about us and only want to eliminate us. Yes, horrible/horrible devastation and loss of life. But dad, sir, those you have faithfully served for 3 years...are your real Enemies>."

"Can't be," Steve expressed in utter amazement. "It was, what, a phony War Game? Playing with death!?" Jurci tried to understand. "He said, 'Nothing to fear but fear itself?' Not real? Then, tell me, for what purpose? Why would British leaders kill their own people?"

"That's the purpose of all wars, dad. There shouldn't be wars. All wars are wrong and primitive and concocted, manufactured, staged in the 'theatre of war.' Every war has been fake, not so goodness triumphs, but so democracy is destroyed. Power-plays, Mafia bosses, so one group dominates another, nothing personal. Wars are unnatural and should have remained in prehistoric times when there wasn't the science and technology to wipe out millions of people."

"You should have been a writer, son."

"I am. I told you..."

"Oh, that's right. My son, the revolutionary writer. Ha."

"What I'm telling you is...Okay, brace yourself for this one. Franklin Delano Rosevelt (Rose of the World, 'velt' is German for 'world') is not who you think he is. Like Mickey Mouse, he's really not the sweet persona that's given to the public. Behind the curtain of closed, private sessions of the U.S.' War Room, he was ordered to enter Europe's War and he did. They told him Pearl Harbor would be bombed and FDR obeyed his orders and commanded that every major ship at sea was to be parked in one spot for

inspection. The perfect target. He was forewarned and allowed the Attack to happen because he had no choice. He had to obey Higher Orders. It was the ideal situation for Britain. Now they got New World America and its war-machine to join the Allies and they expanded their war through global channels. Dad, he's not a good man. The President is a puppet and knew what would happen to you Navy boys at Pearl..."

Words from the Voice cut into Stevie like a knife. He shook. "But. The President won 4 elections, is very beloved and got the country working again with CC Camps. I was, as well as my brothers, part of those camps 3 years ago. That's how we earned some money and survived when there was nothing. And now, yer telling me that all I ever believed in is not true??"

"You're the one, I should say, 'my Steve,' taught me honesty and the right way to be. You knew about State corruption and UNIONS and unfairness almost everywhere you looked: Mafia, labor bosses, protection pay-offs, riots, strikes. That all came way before me. This is nothing new. I'm saying, in the time of my life, life on my planet got worse and worse. This is a parallel Tera and the same thing is happening here. My 'Children of the Future.' I very much worry about what's going to happen to all of us in the days ahead. It seems nothing's getting better and everything's getting worse. Computers and robots were supposed to make everything great, simple and for everything to work far more efficiently..."

"They don't?" Steve Jurci asked.

"It's more like the MACHINE has taken us over and turned us into cold, hard, little cogs of a larger Machine. People don't care like they used to, dad. They're not happy, colorful, independent individuals anymore. They have this insane technology that's dangerous, instead of fantastic technology and

this shit is turning good people into a lot of bad people..."

"Bad people?"

"Yeah, they suck! They're controlled, made mindless by the devices they use. And you thought kids were crazy, I mean in your time, those long-haired, young people were crazy, right? No, man. Youth back then in my time were beautiful, for the most part. Non-violent, smarter, more creative, colorful. Today, no one cares. Can you believe it? Why care when no one else does? Why get smart when no one else is smart? Why do the right thing? They don't know what the right thing is. They're not trained to care or to get it right. Not anymore. They're all the same IDIOTS. But, that is not fair, because we're all victims of our times and environment. People really do have super-potential. But no one programs that fact into their little hearts and heads. It's just a big waste! What humanity could achieve if we were not under the rule of secret fascism."

"Let me see if I got what yer saying? Yer saying, the big 10-year World War was a farse, exactly like smaller conflicts that have happened throughout history? But the real Battle or war, or, or, ultimate truth is: It was done to people as one big...*Double-Cross,* because leaders of the 'free' world aren't the good guys they present themselves to be? They're more like conmen with armies or *criminals,* holding up the whole world with their lies and taking our freedoms away?"

"Ha, ha. Whoever said you were stupid, Stevie?"

"...Some of the guys. I don't know."

"Hey how come you never changed your name to Doug? The father that I knew immediately changed his name. He loved that film. I tried to imagine how hard it was for him to do that. Have everyone call him Doug, like, did you hear what little Stevie wants

us to call him now? They must have laughed at first. Hell, later, even the cousins all knew you as Uncle Doug. You worked at the Post Office and no one knew you as Steve. You were Doug to all your fellow workers. My grandfather changed his name and you did not. Huh."

The boy got choked up again. "I never thought to do that. A postman? Cool."

"I'm an author and artist and I still can't get friends and family to call me by my pen name..."

"What's yer pen name, son?"

"TS Calaban. Tray. That stands for me, you and mom, together."

"That's nice." Steve's expression became serious again. Tears were in his bright, blue eyes. He solemnly asked: "How did I die, son?"

Doug smiled. *"Remember. It was how <u>my</u> dad died. Yer a different man, boy, entirely. Something different will happen to you. But, I'll tell you. He was old, ill, and OH, BY THE WAY, STOP SMOKING CIGARETTES, OLD MAN, OR YOU'LL NEVER LIVE TO BE AN OLD MAN! AND TELL THAT TO YER WIFE TOO! Both of you died along with millions of others way too early! Why? Because England has to have every fucking person in every one of their fucking film noir films LIGHT-UP at the beginning of every damn scene! It made all you little monkeys do the same! So cool, huh? No, cigarettes were never cool! Yer not monkeys, you just look like them! Please, Steve from Tera, please stop smoking cigarettes and get mum to do the same. Got that? Nicotine's the worst drug!"*

Steve raised his hands to his head. "Wow. I feel yer ghost-eyes boring into mine. Yes! We'll quit. I'll make sure of it. Anything so we can have a happy life together."

"That's better. You know, Steve, please don't worry..."

"You didn't answer my question, son? How did I die? How did your father die? I'm curious, mm?"

"Okay. (smile) You died working. You died just where you were born, the old house at 794. Fixing your main recliner-chair in the living room. I came home from my job and there you were collapsed on the floor with the chair upside-down and many of your tools spread around the carpet..."

"Really? That...that almost seems fitting?"

"Yes, dad. You were big on work and you worked until the very end and then your heart gave out. We weren't very affectionate. Mom was. We hugged when we met after not seeing each other for a time. Czechs were colder than Italians. Then the differences between us when I got older. But when I saw you there, dead...I hugged you, kissed you and cried my eyes out."

Precisely at that moment, **Steve Raymond Jurci disappeared into thin air!** The reason? He was never actually there. The Voice, or Spirit of Doug (Tray), was given a dream-wish upon departing his Earthly plane. There were a few things he wanted to tell his young father after the war. Rose's spirit made the encounter happen. It was not an exact fit. The best that could happen was Ghost of Doug that interacted with Ghost of Steve, but it was a Steve from a parallel world, closest one (in frequency) to Doug's world. It was all that was available.

Doug's energy thanked the universe and his mother for the very precious experience. An object in the room suddenly fell from the ceiling and struck the floor. It was the piece of the Kamikaze plane that Steve Yurchey saved as a souvenir and gave to his only son. Then, the room faded out of existence.

In the other world (not Earth), on a planet called Tera, Steve Jurci, seaman 3rd Class, went down with his ship when *a Crimson Wave plane exploded on the deck of his destroyer!* His ship was one of those "dazzle ships" that were painted odd stripes and colors. The camouflage did not fool a solo enemy plane in the South Pacific. The radioed S.O.S. message for assistance to the closest Allied ships was not in time. All sailors onboard died. The number on the side of this particular destroyer was '999.'

Chapter 4:

Rosie Brancati

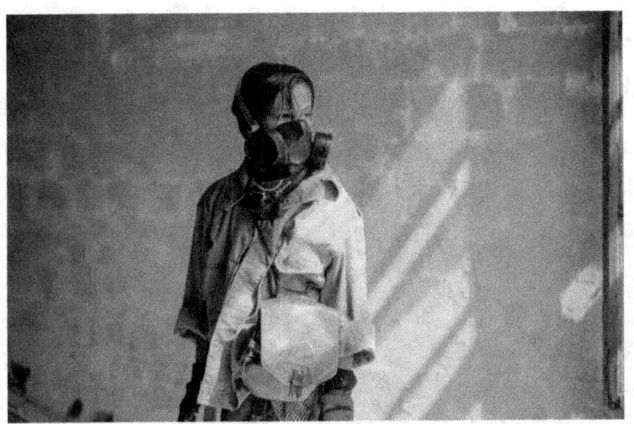

Rosie Brancati was a 12-year old "war-child" that was raised in Sicily amid bombings in her home town of Catania. Her family and most of the buildings were wiped out. She was on her own, a frightened/beautiful girl caught in a hell that no child should ever experience.

Her biggest fears were not German bomber planes or mustard-gas attacks from U-boats that got through the Straits of Gibraltar. Her biggest fears were finding food and rape-gangs finding her. She had been lucky so far. She had witnessed girls younger than her, some of her friends, who had been viciously raped in villages around Catania. Rose hid well. She was always a scavenger and had the nickname "Mouse." But her friends and family and whole world had been gone for months now. She always had a weight problem. She was heavier than most of the girls in her class. Now she was 'thin as a rail.' Rose's last good meal came months ago from a kind, old lady that took care of her.

When the old woman passed and the food was gone, she knew she had to move on and find a way to survive.

She had a girlfriend for a time and they worked in tandem. They'd find a camp within the ruins that only contained a few boys. One would whistle at them from a distance and be *naked*. While the young men chased after the girl, the other ransacked their camp. This worked for a while and sustained them for weeks because the girls ran faster than the boys. But one time when it was Rose's turn to get naked and call to the boys, the first part of the plan worked like a charm, the second part did not. The young men were onto these scavengers that stole food and supplies this way. An armed boy stayed behind. When the girl entered, she was sexually accosted.

Rosie camouflaged herself well and searched the outskirts of Catania for her friend. She never showed and Rose feared that she may have been killed. She moved on and hoped that some *oasis of kindness* might exist somewhere inside the *desert of hell* that surrounded her.

She found one more abandoned, bombed-out building that hardly had a roof. It seemed like a place she could hide the supplies she carried for a time. Possibly, she could make a stand and not be bothered. The latest news was that American soldiers were coming to this southern part of Sicily that had been terribly ravaged by war for many years. She remembered villagers carried happiness in their hearts and believed that the long war would soon end. Then another round of violent explosions hit Catania, the worst of the War, and virtually destroyed the town! From then on, everything changed. There was no home town. The few/surviving people felt shattered, hopeless and were sure the end was very near.

Rosie found one of the hopeful, front pages of a newspaper in a section of the building. In Italian, she said, "I wish. I wish Americans came and saved us..." She carried a soldier's rifle she had found. There were no bullets. She used the rifle for protection anyway. Attackers wouldn't know that it was an empty rifle. She closed her eyes and dreamed of another world, a world that had no wars. *Maybe a handsome Yankee from New York will come to my rescue?* Rose clutched the rifle hard and pressed it tight between her legs. She groaned and fell back onto what represented a blanket. In minutes, she lost herself in dreams and faded into sleep...

***

The girl had a good night's sleep, the first in some time. She had erotic dreams and fantasized that an American soldier made love to her and took away her virginity. She believed she was still in the dream and it was the most incredible experience she ever had...

Until Rose realized she was being raped! The girl screamed! An old, hideous man with a long beard and an awful odor, pushed inside her again and again! She screamed again, and in the next second...

A loud gunshot was heard! The bullet went completely through the old man's head and struck the wall. He fell off of her and out of her, dead.

Rosie cried and shook. She automatically covered herself with her blood-stained clothes. In a moment, she knew she was no longer in danger. She wiped her face and looked up at the man who shot a pistol and ended her pain. He was an American soldier, a handsome young man with blue eyes. With tears in her brown eyes, she smiled at him.

He smiled back. The young man crouched down and stroked

her short, black hair.

Chills ran through her body as he helped her up and onto what passed as a seat.

He spoke words she did not understand: "You'll be alright, kid. We're sweeping this whole area. Didn't you hear? The war is over. We're here to help you now. It'll get better."

The happy girl shined with joy and asked, "Americans sono arriviti?"

He laughed because he understood her. "Ha, ha. Si, si, regazza. Americans have arrived! Ha. Come." He thought to carry her. He didn't when she seemed to be able to walk.

The tall Army man gently held her hand and led her toward outside.

She stopped and said, sweetly, "Dare a te." Her big eyes looked into his. She held his hand tighter. With the other hand, she pulled out a photo of herself.

"For me?" the soldier asked. It was a year-old photo of her and her family before her town was destroyed. (Rose weighed more). "I'm touched...Rose." (written on the back). "I will cherish this and will always remember you. Oh, oh. I have something for you. It's not much..."

She still didn't understand his words. It did not matter. She had stars in her eyes. He said her name.

He gave her a small, metallic object. It was a piece of a German tank that looked cool. "I was going to save this as a souvenir and give it to my kid, if I ever had a kid? Hey, you'll do. For you. Date a te." She understood: a family photo for a piece of an enemy tank. Fair trade.

They walked out of the building and into a better world.

***

Serendipity is a strange thing. It rarely occurred, but sometimes, what almost seemed as an impossibility...actually happens<>.

After the day that a tall Army guy came to the rescue of a frightened Italian girl, and after she was given to nuns in a convent, they never saw each other again...

Until the man walked into 'Crawford Grill' on Wylie Avenue in Pittsburgh's Hill District in 1965. Pittsburgh was once a mecca for JAZZ and jazz musicians in the '30s, '40s, '50s and through the '60s, until the construction of the Civic Arena. The parking lot basically wiped out the Hill and the heart of Iron City's Jazz. Crawford Grill's performers included young Billy Strayhorn, Paul Chambers, Roy Eldridge, Dodo Marmarosa, Errol Garner, Charlie Parker, Thelonious Punk, Muddy Rivers, George Benson and introduced Duke Ellington to the world.

The man heard a lot about this famous club that stood at that spot since the late 1920s and was thrilled he'd be a part of the scene this night. But there was something else in the air that he didn't quite understand. It was as if he was drawn to Wylie Street on this strange night and at this particular time. He thought the 'attraction' might be a new act that he'd soon see and never forget. It was, but there was also something else in the air.

When he got inside, he noticed that his white skin was in about the 5th percentile. He was the outsider that looked in. But the man felt absolutely no prejudices against him. This world, this place, was the center of jazz and had been the center of jazz for decades. The music was for all colors and the tunes were simply divine. If you loved jazz, this was the place to be. He waved to a few white guys at a table through all the cigarette smoke. They smiled and waved back. The black women were gorgeous. The whole atmosphere was intoxicating. You could smell "reefer" being smoked. *This was the night and he knew he was in the exact right place!*

A new act appeared at Crawford's for the first time. There was a wonderful introduction for Joe Harriott's Orchestra and their singer: Rose Marie Brancati. She was a stunning beauty with long black hair and looked a lot like Sophia Loren, only Sophia would be jealous of her body. She sang a new song for the crowd called 'Parallel' with the backing of her 12-piece band. The song was a slow ballad about two star-crossed lovers that were supposed to meet, but never did.

She knocked out the crowd with the romantic, torch song. The white guy in the corner was K-Oed. He'd never seen anyone that beautiful before. And she sounded like a goddess...

Halfway into the song, she walked around the tables, as if she sang it to certain gentlemen in the audience. When she got to the table with the white guy who sat alone, she looked directly into his eyes...

Then she collapsed! Fainted, dead away>.

People gasped, the orchestra stopped the music. Quite a few people rushed to her side and tried to help her.

***

They found a cot and it was used as a stretcher. The next scene was inside the singers' large, dressing room, which contained about a dozen people. The girl came to consciousness as worried fans and band members surrounded her. When Rose Marie was clear-headed, she shooed everyone away, except him. She pointed at him. Everyone else left the room.

"Are you alright?" he asked her as he pulled up a chair close to her chair.

She smiled brightly and gazed into his eyes one more time. She softly asked, "You don't remember me, do you?"

He was bewildered and his face expressed it. "What? We've met before?"

"Ha, ha." She covered her face.

"Don't do that. Yer too beautiful."

With excitement on her face that he felt, she suggested, "There's something you have to see. Ha, I don't believe it, but it's true."

The man was equally excited, grabbed her hands and asked with emotions: "What?!"

Rosie clutched his hand tighter, then reached under her black turtleneck and showed him her pendant: It was a piece of a German tank that he gave her 20 years earlier.

"Huh. Uh. *Rose?*" Automatically, he pulled out his wallet and went to his pictures. There was Rose's happy photo with a few family members.

She gasped and smiled and expressed, "Ugh. All this time?"

He repeated, "All this time. Ah. You sing like a bird. I love birds. And you speak English now, Rose."

Then, she had a thought and said: "Give me that." She grabbed the wallet in a carefree gesture and looked for his identification. "Ah. Now, I know what to call you...*Doug*. Wait a minute, Jurci? You're Italian?"

"Ha, ha, ha." He leaned in and she leaned in and they had their first kiss.

~Unforeseen things sometimes happen that change everything in the world.

Chapter 5:

In Hyperbolic Space

Twelve Lizard Directors from Tera on their way to the Great Conference [1964, thereabouts] in Hyper Space were, of course, cut-off from everything around them and all communications until the end of 'surfing space-way vortexes' and arrival in the Fornax Galaxy.

The 12 had a waking-dream at the very same time. They were forced into a deep meditative state by one of the *Dream-Weavers,* the very first to *Influence* a Reptilian. In this case, the Captain and his crew of eleven were contacted from the Outside, while in hyperbolic space. This was thought to be virtually impossible with a 'zero chance.' Unless under very special circumstances between a traveler that happened to be going your incredible speed and also in your direction.

Captain and crew of Lizards received a message from an entity that called himself/herself 'Gogmagog.' He/she materialized in front of them onboard the Warship's main Council Room as a bright, amorphous, gaseous creature, taller than the Lizards (15 feet). A *visitation* was not what any of the Directors expected.

Teran Directors were 100% oblivious to what went

on back on their Tera and had a million concerns about their decisions. Had the A.I. ruled wisely, compassionately or ruthlessly? Did the A.I. understand the final words at the end of the film '1984'? Was that the right film to learn morality from? Why were all Reptiles everywhere commanded and compelled to attend the Great Meeting? What will they learn? How will Captain and crew change after the important Meeting, on the way back to Tera? What will happen to Terans in the future?

Gogmagog, the Dream-Weaver, entered the Reptile's collective Day-Dream for a moment to help them understand, to answer their questions and lessen their fears. The bright/foggy, Dream-Weaver, mega-telepath had the attention of the Reptiles. The Lizards heard its thoughts, loud and clear:

I am not at liberty to discuss the results, the changes, the conclusions that will be demonstrated and proven to you during your time in Fornax. Only the following am I permitted to relay to you 12 Teran Directors of the Lizard Empire...

I remind you of the limbo you are in and I am in as well...for a time. We cannot touch the Outside and the Outside cannot touch us in the present state. What I know is true, and it is exactly what you will discover to be true in the future. We telepaths are often in frozen conditions where we see terrible events, but are totally helpless in changing them. This I can express to you:

Your A.I., or that particular A.I., was a unique mechanism and not the typical android with expected android reactions. She was corrupted from the Outside. Linked to it, in fact. A wave that originated as Rogue-energy has changed the Game...

Pardon, Gogmagog? the Captain pushed a thought into the entity.

Yes?

Did we error in our construction and in our methods that surrounded the Teran A.I.? Do you mean an Outside source has influenced and corrupted her? Great Seer, you appear to know all things. Can you not answer specific questions?

She/he replied: *I cannot be specific for timeline reasons you must understand. Your question is Non Sequitur or could be considered moot. I cannot express more. The important question is how does the 'end game' play out? Do Terans achieve their destined Wireless World of Tomorrow? Future reality has not crystalized in Time Windows. It remains unclear, uncertain. So far...*

Yes. That was supposed to be the conclusion of our assignment there on the planet after many millennia. Did we succeed? Will we succeed? Was our ultimate goal achieved? We did, inevitably, help the Terans, yes? Can you tell us the final resolution, Great Seer? Or...or, what is most likely to happen?

I reveal to you 12 trustworthy travelers...the answer is YES. But...

But?

In another world, the answer is NO and you were not successful. Both universes or alternatives will merge into a singularity. That result has yet to be seen. The little I have told you can be synthesized down to my feelings or...my GUESS? Do not worry. Everything will work out right in the end. But...in another world, they will not. I hope these thoughts help calm your troubled souls. That was their intent. Gogmagog's strong thoughts and image faded away. The entity was completely gone>.

The Captain turned to his fellow Lizards and said words they understood: "My inclination is that after we hear and see the information broadcast from the Great Conference...it will be such an unbelievable and extraordinary experience for us...that we will never be the same again."

"We have similar feelings, Captain."

Chapter 6:

Films Written by the A.I.

'Things to Come' came before the reign of the A.I. and was a Lizard production from 1934. This was timed perfectly to be pre-War, just prior to the Great War. The story concerned a global war that lasted 20 years and finally ended in a marvelous Utopia. "Lovelier and lovelier." The Lizards' plan gave the people the false sense of hope for tomorrow and their children [temporarily], while only insiders knew the *Winds of a real World War* were soon to come. Very much like the A.I.'s concept of the 1933 New York World's Fair with the famous Perisphere and Trylon centerpiece, and around it, fabulous exhibits of the Future. This was a tease. This was the wrong time for paradise on Tera and the Lizards knew it.

The film's War was pure horror. Countries attacked nations with gas bombs that killed large numbers of Terans. The survivors became the Walking Dead with a *wandering disease.* "Bosses" ruthlessly controlled certain areas and still made war among the ruins. But everything changed when a group of hidden scientists came in with advanced aircraft and cleaned up the small fascist regimes. "Wings Over the World." (McCartney's band: 'Wings'). Then came the fantastic Future where technology and modern machines constructed the threshold of utopia.

Theotocopolos, on many screens and monitors and enormous holographic projections, told the masses: *"What is this progress? What is the good of all this progress onward and onward? We demand a halt, we demand a rest! The object of life is Happy Living. We will not have human life sacrificed to experiment.* (Space Gun shot people into outer space). *Progress is not living..."*

Cabell: "And that voice is sounding to the whole world."

"...What does this Space Gun portend? Make no mistake about it, the Slavery that they put upon themselves today, they will impose tomorrow upon the whole world! Is man never to rest, never to be free? An

end to progress! Make an end to this progress now! Let this be the last day of the scientific age!"

Cabell: "Our fathers and our father's fathers cleaned up the old Order of things because it killed children...it tormented people in vain. It outraged human pride and dignity because it was an ugly spectacle of waste. But that was only a beginning. There's nothing wrong in suffering if you suffer for a purpose. Our Revolution didn't abolish death and danger, it simply made death and danger worthwhile."

"Is there ever to be an age of happiness?"

"Man must go on, conquest beyond conquest. First, this little planet and its winds and ways, and then, all the laws of mind and matter that restrain him. Then the planets about him. At last, out across immensity to the stars. And when mankind has conquered all the deeps of space and all the mysteries of time...still, he will be beginning. If we're no more than animals, we must snatch each little scrap of happiness. It is *this* or *that.* ALL the universe or NOTHING?! Which shall it be? Which shall it be?" {1 or 0?}.

The Machine A.I. for this particular planet Tera, saw the great film with Raymond Massey, Ralph Richardson and Sir Cedric Hardwick...and her circuits *laughed* at foolish human beings. People believed the wonders of the 1933 World's Fair would be true things that would be realities in the near future. In 'Things to Come,' the audiences believed the Hope that was projected upon silver screens and the lights that were illuminated in their hearts. Her circuits *laughed* because, even if the Reptiles suggested that she studied 'Things to Come' instead of '1984,' the result would have been the same. [A remote Dream-Weaver forced the A.I. into the thought, which she contemplated for a short moment]. Then, the A.I. expressed with no doubt at all: "The little animals need to be exterminated."

***

The A.I. was enchanted with the 1927 silent, German expressionist, sci-fi film, 'Metropolis,' directed by Fritz Lang and written by a team of Lizards. It cost the equivalent of 21 million dollars to make and the film was the first feature-length film of that genre. Audiences found it "visually spectacular." The film came under harsh criticism at the time for its anti-capitalist or "Communistic" themes. But the film is now considered "one of the greatest films ever made."

In the future, wealthy industrialists ruled the Super City of Metropolis, with its tall skyscrapers and tremendous landscapes. Fedor, son of the City's Master, idles away his pampered life in a variety of sports and elite "pleasure palaces." Nudity was shown to early theater audiences with beautiful young ladies in 'Gardens of Teran Delights.' Fedor met a lost girl (Maria), who took a group of children to see how rich people lived. Odd encounter between the rich and the poor.

Fedor visited his father's underground complex and found an army of laborers who were very hard at work in long lines. When one shift was over, a massive crew of workers took their place until their shift was over. Then, *an explosion happened!* Fedor became extremely distraught at the accident and the horrific conditions of the lower classes. At one point, he did the job of one of the workers. Their terrible lives were nothing but work, labor which only served the people above who lived in luxury. The dirty, sweaty masses below toiled and operated the Machine that ran functions in the City, continuously. Fedor must have been on Magic Mushrooms because he *hallucinated* that the Machine ate rows and rows of workers that walked into its mouth! The scene was unexpected and had stunning effects as if the Machine was Moloch in the bowels of the Underworld? Or something out of hellish Bosh paintings? The masses lived the mindless lives of slaves, while rich industrialists and their families had everything they desired.

Later, after he realized his father's indifference to the worker's awful conditions, he joined the revolt against his father. The explosion was not an accident, but a bombing. He met the magician-scientist Rotwang in a brothel, the revolution's leader. In the meantime, Maria (like an angel) addressed a large group of people and claimed that a "mediator" will come and solve the problems between the Ruling Class and the workers. Was she psychic? Fedor fell in love with sweet Maria and he believed that he was the Mediator that she prophesied.

Fedor was betrayed by Rotwang who turned Maria's influence and charm into EVIL. He saw how she moved the masses and used her. He transformed her into a dark persona named "**Hel**." She was Rotwang's puppet and led the masses not to peace, but into *war with the upper class!* An upside-down Pentagram was featured on the wall, pointed down. [Few realized its meaning in 1927].

When the A.I. viewed the film, she was delirious with glee as enraged workers burned Maria at the stake, and underneath, **it was a** (bald) **female ANDROID!** The Machine felt that it was Fate that she had absorbed this film. *She was Hel.* She was the "living machine" of Anarchy that ruled without feelings, without compassion. The A.I. was *sorry* that the robot, the instigator of Hate and War, perished in the film. Rotwang fell to his death. Fedor became the Mediator between management and workers and the story ended happily. *PUKE!* The A.I. was sure that a World Metropolis like in the film or at the end of 'Things to Come,' would never happen in real life. Utopia remained a dream; it was only in her films.

***

The A.I. had written, produced and pushed many of

her movies since 1957. She allowed her top General* and harshest critic [#7] to put out a film for the masses. He accepted when he learned that the A.I. would not change or edit it.

[*To clarify, the Lizards left Tera for the Great Meeting in Fornax and so did ALL of the Lizards who left their planets and attended the Conference. The 12 Generals left behind as Teran Council members, with the 13th Vote being the A.I., were *clones.* 12 Lizard clones and the "Chairwoman" ran everything on Tera].

#7 took over and controlled the body of Ray Bradbury. Bradbury was a unique member of the Illuminati. Rarely had the society or *Machine* come across a real/natural genius. "Genius" and "talent" were almost exclusively rigged, made, forced - material was given to "stars." Ray was different. He needed no teams of ghostwriters to fill his 'content.' He was a brilliant, self-taught, writing-machine. But, it was the Lizard "under the skin" of Ray Bradbury that wrote 'Fahrenheit 451.' The clone's concept was a masterpiece and mimicked '1984' in many ways.

In the story, most books were banned because they contained a zillion things that the fascist State did not approve of. In '1984,' the State eliminated individual words: If you got rid of words like 'freedom' and 'liberty,' then next generations would not know what freedom and liberty were. In '451,' whole books were declared too radical, too subversive, too much of what opposed the dictates of the State or New Order. 'Firemen' didn't put out fires (since all buildings were fireproof), they BURNED BOOKS! Religious books, philosophic books, romance novels, books of science-fiction and fantasy, dramas/fictions, new wave arts, nearly every type of book imaginable. Except black and white, straight-forward (edited) historical documentaries or technical science manuals of basic information.

Libraries were a thing of the past in fireman Montag's world. The main character, along with other firemen, rode in a large/red fire truck to homes and places they suspected people hoarded these outlawed books. Citizens were stopped in the street and searched as if they had no rights at all. Severe penalties and even the death penalty were attached to anyone who broke the Law and possessed books. Montag fell in love with the Julie Christie-character in the film, which paralleled the love story inside of '1984.'

At one point, someone snitched on an old lady whose house was essentially a library of her precious books. Firemen invaded her home in a violent raid and searched each floor in the woman's house. They piled up her books into a big heap and *set fire to them!* Montag witnessed that the old woman climbed on the pile of books and *she was torched right along with them!*

This intrigued the young fireman: The woman felt so

strongly about her books that she died with them as if she could not bare to live without her books? What was so special about books? What was in them that made citizens defy the Law under severe penalties? He wanted to find out.

During a few of the firemen's raids, when he had chances to be alone, he hid a few paperbacks inside his clothes. Montag was always careful. In time, he accumulated quite a collection. He lived a lonely life and was able to cover this *interest,* almost an obsession, for contraband material. He had to know what was it that made books so wrong and verboten? His collection included:

'To Kill a Mockingbird' by Harper McGee.
'The Grapes of Wrath' by John Steinbeck.
'The Catcher in the Rye' by J.D. Sallinger.
'Gone with the Wind' by Margaret Mitchel.
'Animal Farm' by George Orwell.
'Brave New World' by Aldous Huxley.
'The Hobbit' by J.J.R. Tolkien.
'A Clockwork Orange' by Anthony Burgess.
'The Call of the Wild' by Jack London.
'The Martian Chronicles' by Ray Bradbury.
'Catch-22' by Joseph Keller.
'The Masks of Time' by Robert Silverberg.
'Lolita' by Vladimir Nabokov.
'New Men and the New World' by TS Caladan.
'The Good Earth' by Robert Bloch.
'Crimson Wave' by Ernest Hemingway.
'No Free Lunch' by Chris Henderson.

Montag found in them: Words of freedom. Words of color and wild flights of imagination. Words of love and feelings. He had time in the evenings and read the books. He read almost all of them in the months that he had stolen books. The man wanted more and more books, like they were an addictive drug. Later, he shared his secret with the Julie Christie-character and discovered she was part of an underground group of "book-people." She took him to their community in the country, away from the city, where these good people lived a simple life.

"Book-People" chose one book that they related to and was close to. Then they "became the book." They memorized the entire book! Word-for-word, they'd recite it for young and old so the ideas in books never died. Firemen could burn every book, but the voices of freedom will continue. Books and emotions will live-on in people. Eternal. Upon old age or when very ill, book-people recited their book to a young person who also committed it to memory. In this way, the rich, literary, spectrum of the human race was preserved.

This was the way the story was written by the Reptile Bradbury, #7, who was given the opportunity by the A.I. to "put something out for the masses." Seven was proud of 'Fahrenheit 451,' (temperature paper burns) and his inspirational ending that made the book and movie very successful on Tera.

The important and very secret factor was: There was

a group of *Rogue Lizards* that were Negative Energy and turned a decent Lizard into one badass motherfucker! Some of the 12 +Lizards (clones) had turned to the Dark Side...

In another universe, one of an infinite number, a different Reptile Bradbury (-) wrote a completely different story and it had no sweet ending:

The Julie Christie-character, at first, pretended to be a rebel spy and book-lover when she realized Montag stole and read the contraband books. But the ending of this '451' was not too different from the ending of '1984.' It ended BADLY! She always worked for the State and never loved Montag. Thanks to her efforts as a spy who acted as a Book-Person, she found the community and discovered what they were up to. Montag was shot dead. Every available firetruck raided the village of book-people and torched everything! No happy ending><.

***

The A.I. placed a "happy ending" in one of the first films that the Machine designed: '12 Angry Men,' credited to Rose Reginald and starred Henry Fonda. [Hollywood clue: Whenever a *gender* was in the title of a film, it was primarily played by actors of the opposite gender]. The film was a dramatic courtroom battle directed by Sydney Lumet. The story explored the deliberations of a jury in a homicide trial, in which a dozen men decided the fate of a teenager accused of murdering his abusive father. In the beginning, the jury was nearly unanimous and concluded that the youth was guilty of the crime. One man dissented (Fonda) and declared him "not guilty." He sowed a seed of *reasonable doubt*. Eventually, he convinced the other jurors and they supported a unanimous "not guilty" verdict. A happy conclusion because the boy was innocent of the charge.

Why was the A.I. eager to make this film and had one of her top New York stooges direct it? Answer: She gave the masses *the idea that one man can turn the tide against a sea of madness or a tsunami of wrongfulness~*. No, they couldn't. The Machine made sure that there would be no future uprises against her Authority. There would be no revolutions counter to her Will. But people were molded to believe that "they could FIX the planet and right all the injustices in the real world." No, not at all. That false concept was only placed in her movies and would never be a part of the physical world, under her control. The A.I. made the Law and her inhuman minions obeyed it and so did the smaller slaves under them.

The A.I. did the very same thing to the whole planet with the Peace and Love '60s Movement. The Machine created great, colorful music at the time. The A.I. produced the wild, positive changes that occurred politically, the colorful fashions, the art, the Happenings and even fabricated the Love that was felt in the air! The reason was: So that the world will never have peace, love, security, balance, and higher learning ever again! But Terans will be made to think that *united as one* will bring about a better tomorrow. '12 Angry Men' had a similar purpose when it gave audiences the false sense that *they made a difference.*

***

'Spartacus' (1960) was another film project conceived by the A.I. The role went to young Kirk Douglas [from a tranny-family, like the Fondas, etc.]. Douglas was forced to purchase the entire project after arguments with the original director, Tony Mann (woman). He was urged to have Stanley Kubrick as the director. The story concerned Spartacus, one of the slaves, who led a revolt against the Roman Republic. ["I am Spartacus!" We are all Spartacus]. Once again, the popular theme stressed heavily in future films: "People can rise up against the State and overthrow an evil empire!" Once again, the cold truth of reality: No, you cannot.

***

In 1958, American theaters showed what was considered one of the greatest films of all time and certainly the greatest Christmas film of all time: *'It's a Wonderful Life.'* Why Jimmy Stewart in the lead role?

He had been the highest-ranked Actor in the Great War (and killed for Satan the most), therefore, he'd be America's Darling in this film shown every Christmas. This was, once more, a deceptive move on the part of the A.I. She portrayed a classic story (same with Scrooge and the Grinch) that pulled at everyone's heartstrings and brought many to tears. Was Life wonderful? Yes. But that was not how it would be for the Children of the Future. One more *false sense* that living was beautiful, living was divine. It could be Heaven on Tera. The whole time, the Machine had plans on her 'drawing board' to make it 'A Horrible Life' for Terans.

***

The films credited to Alfred Hitchcock were not directed by the Master director. He never wrote a play, a screenplay, a movie, a story or even one word of what was credited to the "great man." Again, out of England. He was not a man, yet the "actor" himself pretended that he was a horny pervert that lusted after his blonde, leading "actresses." It was an act. Stories abound where HitchCOCK "could not keep it in his pants" and came on to the famous blondes he lusted after. Not true. He was a heavy, bald woman and the blonde girls were really feminized boys. Wasn't Grace Kelly, later Queen of Monaco, a clue? Alfred was given the American anthology series, 'The Alfred Hitchcock Hour,' and he was thoroughly embarrassed by the production, which received great reviews. The *man* was even against the idea of a walk-on signature in his films. He never wanted to be bothered with interviews, like many others, and the whole *lie* of his celebrity. The public was given the impression that Hitchcock was one of the Masters of Horror. Inside his large framework, he was actually an easily-scared, little girl.

***

'Forbidden Planet' (1959) was a high-budget, sci-fi, mega-film very much ahead of its time with Robbie the Robot and included fantastic special-effects. It starred veteran actor, Walter Pigeon, Leslie Nielson and Ann Francis. *Forbidden Planet* is considered one of the greatest sci-fi films of all time and compared to Shakespeare's 'The Tempest.' The film was selected for preservation by the U.S. Library of Congress for its "cultural, historical and aesthetic significance."

In the story, a United Planets starship arrived at Altair 4 to discover what happened to an expedition sent 20 years earlier. They were warned not to land by Morbius, a survivor of the previous mission. But the Commander ignored the order, landed and found the planet's only inhabitants: Morbius, his daughter Altaira and the Robot. The Commander was told that a "planetary force" killed all the others of the last mission except for himself. His daughter was born after the tragedy and then her mother passed away. The Commander and his men thought it was suspicious that this Monster, or whatever it was, hadn't returned in 20 years and left him and his daughter alone?

But when some of the crew showed signs of affection for Altaira, the "creature" returned as an invisible, unstoppable force and killed a few of the men! Later, Morbius took the Commander and his main officers to an incredible underground facility whose area was many miles in length. They learned of the Krell, prehistoric natives that developed fantastic technologies and built the amazing underground facility. Then suddenly, mysteriously, they died. The crew was shown a machine that increased mental capacity. Morbius had used it on himself many times; he tinkered together Robbie the Robot. The mind-machine was responsible for much of the super-tech items inside their living quarters.

The climax of the film was when Morbius realized that *he created the creature!* It was a "Monster from the Id." His Id. He had found the mind-device, used it against the others of the first mission and killed them! Then he had forgotten that he'd killed them. Now the tranquil world with his daughter he had created was threatened and that was why his Monster returned. In another attack by the invisible creature, all hell was about to break loose...But Morbius fell dead because of the power or by the terrible realization that hid in his subconscious. The Monster was dead also, and never returned. Happy ending: The Commander and starship crew took Altaira to Tera, a world she'd never seen before. Robbie drove.

The A.I.'s message in her film was a vague one, hardly understood by people in the 20th Century. Forbidden Planet's message was for aliens or for Terans of the future who might build such devices that <u>made thoughts REAL</u>. In the story, the Krell had risen to such mental heights that their thoughts were materialized. But the Krell *destroyed themselves* because of this great power. In other words: Don't even bother materializing human thoughts and making them real. Human thoughts were only negative, dangerous and very destructive.

Not True. All one had to do was control their thoughts, which any intelligent lifeform should be able to do. It wouldn't be Monsters from the Id, then...it would be **Beautiful, Wonderful Things from the Id!** This had to do with the nature of the human being. Were they gods or were they always in error, doomed for failure and occupied a low level on the Spectrum of Life? The A.I. Machine always placed humans on the low end. The A.I. Machine was wrong.

She put the same theme in one of her original Star Trek episodes that involved an Amusement Planet for higher minds. *Thoughts were Made Real.* Those on the planet had to control their thoughts or reality got out of hand.

***

'Lord of the Rings' had always been, according to the Lizards, not a myth. Not a fantasy about a kingdom called 'Middle-Tera.' It was a tribute to the god of the Underworld, *Saturn.* The 'Rings' were the planet Saturn's rings. 1-eye 'Sauron' was the same as evil 'Saturn,' and evil 'Satan' and even the evil red 'Santa.'

The A.I. learned about the Power Ring in 'The Hobbit' and in the trilogy that followed. She understood its significance, the real meaning, which flew over most people's heads (outside of a few *tripping* hippies). Fantastic Powers of the Mind! [same as with the Krell]. What incredible things can be done with semi-full usage of the mind's potential, 70%, 80% or even 90%! Truth is, and super intelligent species know this: Terans do not use "10%" of the mind, as had been reported. They only used a fraction of 1% of 1% of what brain-power could actually do! If 10% of true potential was utilized, *humans could move mountains with the power of the mind!*

In 'Lord...,' when a person placed the Power Ring on their finger, their mental powers expanded/enhanced by a factor of a million! Their Mind ruled any situation and could blast large armies to smithereens. This was always supposed to have symbolized LSD and its real effects on people. Dr. Allen Hoffman of the Dynatech Corporation had honestly "stumbled upon" rye-ergot bread molds that first produced LSD-25. He and J.R.R. Tolkien were good friends and Tolkien was a willing test-subject for the powerful psychedelic.

Tolkien was one more British front-man who took credit for what he never did. *He was a bad writer* and never learned to write a proper sentence. But he possessed an amazing imagination. His scribbles on paper, napkins, *anything,* were given to teams of ghost writers and they were the ones who actually made the novels what they were, not J.R.R. Yet the Hobbits, the Orks, the Elves and the whole bizarre world of Middle-Tera originated from his "fueled" mind.

When interviewed and asked about his high popularity among hippies and about LSD, Tolkien always denied and pleaded: *coincidence.* He lied and said the story characters came from his dreams. He also claimed he knew nothing of LSD and was simply pleased that the younger generation enjoyed his work.

***

One more novel credited to Ray Bradbury was 'The Martian Chronicles,' which Ray had said was not a sci-fi book and that he "wasn't a sci-fi writer." He called it a "Greek Tragedy." In this particular case, Lizards had nothing to do with the book and televised mini-series with Rock Hudson. The Machine or the A.I. created the story. No one got the joke except the A.I. It was a sharp slap in the face to a real Martian race that acted very much like the real Venusian race of people on Venus. [Martians and Venusians obeyed the #1 Directive and did not interfere. Nikola Tesla spoke to and spoke of both alien (but human) civilizations to the World Press, that he had contacted them. But very few people believed Tesla].

In the story, the Martians only had their *minds* as defense weapons against any type of invasion. They made illusions for the Teran astronauts that landed. The men saw their mothers or fathers or other loved ones that had long been dead. *Was Mars heaven?* The men observed whole towns they were familiar with back on Tera. The illusions were done so the Martians had the opportunity and sat down to dinner and eventually poisoned the invaders. [*"You couldn't hide the air"*]. The invaders were actually colonists who had no idea that Mars was inhabited.

The high insult was: *Modern Martians would never do what was done in 'The Martian Chronicles.'* They would never murder colonists. Martians, real ones, are human, not weird aliens. They would welcome people from Tera who, after so many millennia, found their way back home. Mars was the original home for one group of human beings. That's why there are pyramids and a mile-long *face* on Mars that looked straight up into the sky. [*Historical note: When ancient warrior Martians destroyed the 5th planet and, as a result, created the Asteroid Belt...the recoil from the Particle Beams *decimated Mars, turned it red with radiation!* Some survivors made it to Tera and built Atlantis in the Atlantic Ocean. Atlantis was a Martian colony. Terans are Martians]. Today, Martians would *love* if Teran brothers and sisters had returned to the mother-planet. They wouldn't have killed them.

Also, Martians were people who appeared like people, beautiful people with advanced technology. *They have Long Hair!* -Bradbury (Lizard) portrayed them as bald, murderous, very low, almost primitive in their thoughts and fears. A Martian husband's jealousy when his psychic wife fell for "York," an in-coming astronaut. The very idea that sex, lust, revenge, marital rage and murder were the motivations of present-day Martians were horrible insults to the intelligent people on the 4th planet. They are honorable and durable people that stayed on Mars and survived nasty conditions for thousands of years. And here was how they were *back-stabbed* by a Teran Machine that was far worse than any Martian Enemy in her ridiculous movies. Yet, the A.I. was proud of her deed and her private joke.

***

The A.I. had always lied and fooled the masses with movies, television, music, sports and about everything. She made (forced) a particular TV show upon America that was highly popular and greatly beloved: 'I Love Lucy.' The general public did not know that the title really meant: *'I Love Lucifer.'* It was subliminal for Terans to love the Devil. Who was cast? Lucille Ball, redhead. Why? She was given the perfect name. 'Baal' was an evil god worshipped by Canaanites and also called Moloch. The 4 main stars of the show were not the gender that the public believed. 'I Love Lucy' begat endless other shows with Lucy and *her* brood. No matter what TV channel or time or year, there was some Lucy Show shoved down the throats of fans (outsiders). This was completely because of an A.I. Controller "Chairwoman" behind the scenes that wanted to invert the whole world!

'Gilligan's Island' was another show where the actors all came from the secret tranny pool. Very popular and seen everywhere in re-runs. Such sexual tension on the fake island. More of the A.I.'s joke pushed on American people and the world. These type of shows and movies set the pattern: *That was acting!* Love scenes or hot scenes between tranny Alpha males and tranny Alpha-females were the A.I.'s specialty. The more sexuality and sex were pushed, the more it was pushed by the wrong gender. They were sexually reversed. It was hilarious to the Machine. The Machine loved *her* handiwork and made complete fools out of simple audiences. Later, popular and very well-written shows like 'Cheers,' 'Seinfeld,' 'Friends,' 'Fraser,' 'Curb...' were exclusively Tranny Showcases.

***

Then came 'Myra Breakinridge,' a book and film not written by Gore Vidal. Gore was the controversial NY (secret) trans-gender that was given credit for 'Myra' by the A.I., as well as her other books. The story: Myron Breakinridge (Rex Reed) flew to Europe for a sex-change operation and was transformed into gorgeous Myra Breakinridge (Raquel Welch). Every main star in the film was a *tranny* because the A.I. did all the casting of Hollywood films that had Code and messages and were highly pushed in the Media. This is precisely what the Machine wanted: A film about trans-genders that completely deceived the public. How could people still not know? *That was Hollywood, that was Entertainment or the Show,* under Lizard A.I. Control: the more you lied and deceived the innocent, unsuspecting public, the more you were rewarded. Myra Breakinridge's cast:

John Huston, Farah Fawcet, John Carradine, Jim Backus, Andy Devine, Roger C. Carmal, Tom Selleck, etc. Entire lives of countless numbers of celebrities, especially top celebrities with names that most people know, have been planned - programmed - scripted... Not because of their talent, but because of their ACT that fooled the public from the earliest ages. If you were a well-known celebrity, there was a 90% chance you were not the gender that you appeared. Shirley Temple (Black Temple) was a very well-trained and very sexually abused, little boy. There were low-level Extras in movies that were also in the Secret Order of trans-genders. That's how big stars started. How did they get parts? How did actors get movie part after movie part and careers were jet-propelled, while others (non-trannies) struggled? Why were actresses called "actors"? Why did famous people always partner with other famous people? Did they know the Big Secret? How did actors' names get above the title of the movie in the credits? How did they get their job on a television show or their own show with their name in the title? Not because the theatricals were special talents; it was because jobs were (almost) always given to the same pool of people in the A.I.'s Secret Tranny Club. Every prime face we saw in 'Myra' as well as photos from past celebrities (Elvis/Marilyn Monroe), were famous trans-genders and general audiences had no clue.

Mae West was an extremely old Drag-Man. Her sex and genitalia jokes were endless, way too much and over the top. To force and force dick, pussy and fucking jokes should have told audiences this was a Tranny-Festival. *That's what the movie was about!* Only Insiders knew the truth: the primary cast all had sex-changes in real life and were on hormones of the gender they appeared. The film's climactic moment was when hot, sexy Myra (Raquel) jumped on a table and revealed what they had done to him. The camera only caught his/her rear as she showed off his/her new 'package' to the lustful, old men on the other side.

In later years, Raquel Welch was made to reveal *her* impressions of working with Mae ("Come up and see me sometime") West on 'Myra.' She pretended (made to) she didn't know that Mae was a man, but *she suspected it.* More B.S. to the public~. Fact was (and only an unfeeling, cold, sexless Machine would impose this) everyone has been "Ellen Paged." Ellen Page was one of the few "actors" allowed to finally admit the truth to the world: She's always been a boy. Shouldn't he give back the female awards? It's not that mostly all famous people are gay and perverted, it's that mostly all famous people have been trans-gendered...and outside-people don't know because they have not been told. They're not in the Secret Club.

***

In 1963, Stanley Kramer (surprisingly, not a tranny) directed his comedy debut with a super all-star cast that included: Spencer Tracy, Edie Adams, Sid Caesar, Milton Berle, Jimmy Duranti, Jonathan Winters, Buddy Hacket, Ethel Merman, Mickey Rooney, Phil Silvers, Terry-Thomas, Dick Shawn, Dorothy Provine, Barrie Chase, William Demarest, Andy Devine, Selma Diamond, Jim Backus, Ben Blue, Joe D. Brown, Peter Falk, Norman Fell, Stan Freberg, Leo Gorcey, Sterling Holloway, Don Knotts, Evert Edward Horton, Zazu Pitts, Mike Mazursky, Marvin Kaplin, Arnold Stang, Madlyn Rue, Carl Reiner, Jesse White, Queen Donovan, Jack Benny, Bill Talbert, Doodles Weaver, Allen Michaels and the Three Stooges.

Every comedian from the past was only in 'Mad, Mad, Mad, Mad World' because they were trans-gendered stars from the beginning and had their careers handed to them. Why was the Treasure that the actors were *mad* after, buried under a "Big W"? It was one more joke by the A.I. that not even the actors were aware of. It stood for **WAR**! Subliminally, people were supposed to be *mad, ga-ga and* support any war the MACHINE produced for the world of Tera. [Before the Great Re-Set, the film's title was longer: 'It's a Mad, Mad, Mad, Mad, Mad World'].

***

'Fail Safe' was a Cold War thriller film from 1964 directed by (NY stooge) Sidney Lumet and not written by Eugene Wheeler. The A.I. Machine desired to play with nuclear destruction again and thought of a clever way to do so. Would the plot in 'Fail Safe' be a precursor to a real situation in the world? She considered the possibility as a first stage to her WW2 plan. How could the A.I. get the leaders of a country to drop an atomic bomb on their own country? Well, let's say a Russian plane went off course over U.S. airspace and along with a glitch in the communications network, American computers misinterpreted the foreign plane and it was identified and viewed as a *sudden attack!* Automatically, a "Group 6" squad of "Vindicator" bombers was ordered to *attack Moscow with atomic bombs!* Once the mistake was realized by NORAD, all attempts to rescind the orders were jammed. U.S. fighter planes were sent to shoot down the three Vindicator bombers. Two of them were shot down, but the lead bomber was far ahead of the others and continued into Russian space. The U.S. fighter planes ran out of fuel over the Arctic Circle and plunged into the sea. The lead bomber received counter-orders to not proceed to Moscow and not deploy the Bomb. But, the aircraft was also given valid orders that checked out and directed them to proceed to the target. [The film was similar to her 'Dr. Strangelove' film].

Nothing stopped the fact that **Moscow and millions of Russians were atom bombed off the face of Tera!** Losses were staggering and were 100% due to computer error and not human error. At the height of the Cold War, now what?

President of the U.S. (Henry Fonda) was advised that the Russians would absolutely counter-attack with their full arsenal of nuclear missiles. Tera was on the brink of World War Two by the Superpowers! Will it be the ultimate annihilation that Terans had feared since the beginning of the nuclear age?

A.I. wondered: When the Lizards returned, what would they think of her 'Fail Safe' (ironic title) actually happening in the real world? Such a "Fail Safe" plan could be initiated to kickstart another World War? Would the Reptiles go for it? She'd play the film for them and suggest the possibility at the end of the year. That would be, of course, if the creators were aligned with her depopulation plans?

The climax of the film was simply divine in the mechanical eyes of the Android A.I. The U.S. President (Fonda, of all people) pleaded over the Hotline to the Kremlin that, at all costs, the Prime Minister must not counter with nukes, which automatically would set off more U.S. nukes to Russia. This must not happen for the sake of the planet. There cannot be a radioactive planet and a Nuclear Winter left for our children and their future. The U.S. President would order that AN ATOM BOMB BE DROPPED ON NEW YORK CITY! In this way, the madness terminated here and the destruction would not result in the end of the world...

"Would President Cuban nuke New York City? Maybe...if asked to?" the A.I. said to herself.

***

A 1974 film that was "adapted from a Kurt Vonnegut short story" really originated from an idea written by the A.I.,'Sirens of Titan.' The story concerned a giant Robot, a wayward/single traveler whose spaceship went off course and crashed on Saturn's moon, Titan. The Robot's name was Salo. It had acquired, in crystal storage cells, the sum total of knowledge from the Bengazzi and best specimens of the people.

Salo immediately transmitted an emergency beacon back to its home planet, lightyears away. Its ancient culture neared End Times. The giant Robot's crucial mission was to find a suitable planet for colonization. The 4th planet in the system it had entered appeared as if it had the right conditions for the Bengazzi. Then, a strong/magnetic Solar Wind changed everything and forced a crash landing on Titan. *Storage units that held more than 10 thousand human specimens in cryo-chambers were completely destroyed!* Libraries of knowledge and technology to begin Life on a new world were demolished in the crash! Seeds for hundreds of farms were rendered unusable! It seemed as though the Bengazzi Race, a rich culture of humanity with such tremendous knowledge, would be lost forever.

Salo utilized a long-range scanner device and observed that there was a fairly primitive civilization on the third planet. They were pre-industrial, violent, superstitious, ignorant, human beings. The Robot wanted to help them. Salo couldn't restart the Bengazzi people, but maybe there was a way it could guide these "Terans"? In its language, the word meant 'ground people.'

Ages passed and over the scanner device, Salo saw the fruits of its efforts. The Machine remotely aided the Terans whereby they made great agricultural, technical and spiritual strides. A modern civilization was the end result, a world that avoided wars, social injustices and was a beautiful place to live for all citizens.

The dark film was far from the sweet Vonnegut

story, above. A.I. believed it conjured a clever twist for the film: There was no civilization on the third planet, outside of the one the Builders "planted" from a distance of billions of miles. [?] The scanner device was used to receive indirect messages from home (via the 3rd planet) to Salo, from time to time. Lonely Salo was stranded on a desolate Titan for a very long period.

The whole purpose of the human race, in the changed version, was to act as a means of *visual-communications* between lost wanderer on Titan and its home planet. For example, the Roman Coliseum was actually a round symbol of Peace in the Bengazzi language, which told Salo to "be calm, we know the situation." Much later, which was a short time to Salo, the Great Wall of China was constructed. When Salo viewed Tera and saw the Wall, it understood the structure (when seen from above) really meant: "Hang tight, rescue ship has been launched." Still later, Florida's Overseas Highway connected 44 tropical islands from mainland Florida to Key Largo. The long, white highway with a deep/blue background was the final communication sent to the old, giant Robot. The translation was: "Rescue ship was lost in an ion storm and we do not have the funds to send another ship. Sorry."

Horrible and sad ending for a Robot that audiences were invested in for 1 hour and 49 minutes. But what of the human race? Look what the change did: It made the human race MEANINGLESS. We were nothing but alien code to contact some robot around a moon of Saturn? ["We're more than magnetic ink," a line from The Moody Blues]. That was the purpose of life? No God, no plan, no paradise in this world or in the next? Why bother to live a human life? Without purpose, everything was just meaningless. Once again, the Machine was very proud of herself. 'Sirens of Titan' will have a significant (-) Influence>.

***

In 1975, the A.I. could not help herself. She cooked up a nifty way to change everything *in the opposite direction* again. 'The Planet of the Apes' story was given to author Pierre Boulle, although he did not write it and had to accept it [he was outraged, insulted] as a part of his canon of books. The well-known film was an exact version of the popular novel where *Apes evolved from Men!*

Charlton Heston was the A.I.'s clear choice for the lead role since he played 'Moses' 'Michelangelo,' 'Judah Ben-Hur,' 'El Cid,' 'King Henry,' 'Cardinal Richelieu,' 'Mark Anthony,' 'John the Baptist,' 'Jesus Christ,' 'God' and that guy in 'Soylent Green.' The Machine figured that audiences would follow him wherever he went, even with his known great love of guns.

The idea was for people to believe humans

originated from primates such as Australopithecus, Homo-Erectus, Cro-Magnon. [Same as in the film '2001']. 'Planet of the Apes' where intelligent Apes came after a modern human age, still emphasized human beginnings on Tera as primitive and primates were our ancestors. No way. She knew the truth of a super high-tech age in Tera's distant past (Atlantis, Egypt, Inca, Maya, India, etc.) and the A.I.'s schools/colleges for common people were nothing but contradictions and lies. That B.S. was for her "vermin rats," not intellectuals or the more enlightened Illuminati. Who built the very ancient pyramids and moved those massive monoliths? Not primitives and not aliens. The answer is: Human Gods drove saucer-Chariots ("vimanas"), the Ancient Astronauts, super-Indians, their forefathers. These historic truths and the real flow of History were kept from the general public. The A.I. always pushed the concept of primitive, stupid cavemen and cavewomen and wrong views of what dinosaurs and "mythical" creatures really were. She knew better and kept Occult knowledge for her elite minions as they advanced up secret masonic levels.

Audiences took for granted that today's complex age came from a simple time period, without understanding the real truth: if you went much further back in time, the prehistoric Teran world became very complex and high-tech. It was the super potential of Humankind and the original Greatness of the First Human Civilizations on

Tera that the A.I. had cancelled and forced in its place: the lie of primates, cave-people, simple tools, dinosaurs and "mythical" creatures.

***

In 1962, the extremely controversial film 'The Manchurian Candidate,' directed by John Frankenstein, was forced into the public's consciousness when the production by the A.I. hit theaters. The film concerned 'Mind-Control,' *brainwashing,* and how the U.S. and its "enemies" created perfect assassins that had no memory of what they did. A card in the deck (Queen of Diamonds) was used as a *trigger* that motivated the hypnotized "sleeper agent" who then, automatically, performed the assassination. The film starred tranny Frank Sinatra *who had trouble getting the film made. He called his tranny friend, President Kennedy, and the film was made.* [All lies, for the Press and the Media-Machine].

The A.I. told the public the exact truth in a film. This was what was done in the real world by the A.I.'s many minions in the CIA and NSA. This was how "They," the spidery tentacles of the Machine, got away with their bloody crimes against those that the Elites eliminated. The answer as to *why* expose (and plan a remake) how the dirty deeds were done, was obvious. Very few citizens, outside of Conspiracy Theorists, would ever believe that the story was basically true.

'The Stepford Wives' was a 1972 "feminist horror" novel and film, not written by Ira Levin. It was written by the Machine that was very interested in something that *pushed* her 'Women's Movement' lightyears ahead. The A.I. thought that when she shot down the Equal Rights Amendment (equal pay for women doing the same jobs as men) and had it rejected each time it was proposed, *that would get the ladies really angry!* The effect was minimal. This was a time long before women doctors, women police officers and women soldiers. The Android "Chairwoman" found it difficult to kickstart her Woman's Movement in these early days. The film 'Stepford Wives' was one more attempt.

The character Joanna (Katherine Ross), wife and young mother, suspected that the wives in Stepford had changed from free-thinking, intelligent individuals into compliant wives dedicated solely to homemaking and women who only (mechanically) served their husbands. In time, she got more disturbed as lady friends seemed to be automatons. Joanna knew that a few of them were feminine-activists in the past. *What happened? Did something poison or brainwash the wives of Stepford? Why was her husband gone in the evenings at meetings "with the boys"?*

She discovered that the leader of the Men's Club was a Disney engineer. Along with other technicians in the little group, they made life-like robots of their wives and then disposed of the real ones. The A.I. Machine was disappointed by passive women in the theaters and wanted them pissed. Very pissed. The film still did not have the full negative effect that the A.I. thought it would have on society.

It was followed up by the comedy film: 'How to Murder Your Wife,' with Tony Curtis and Verna Lisi. Curtis' character was a cartoonist and he enjoyed his Bachelor-life in New York City. He attended a friend's party, got drunk and *married* a beautiful, blonde, Italian girl who popped out of a cake! The next day, he was angry. A divorce was not possible because of her immigration status. He was stuck and in his cartoons, he drew different ways to Murder Your Wife. She then disappeared and there were all the signs present that he killed her via the "glopada glopada" machine (cement mixer). He was arrested and appeared in court, even though her body was not found. The jurors were men. His clever lawyer got him acquitted when he said: *"Hey, boys, find this man Not Guilty and you will scare the panties off every wife in the country! They will obey your every wish, so afraid that you'd kill them and get away with it."* The ploy worked. Stanley was pronounced Not Guilty. His wife appeared in the happy ending and the couple fell in love. Predictable. Not so happy an end when her Italian mother moved in with them. This film and other movies, as well as Feminist news items, did not ignite the Sex War she planned. A.I. realized that the "woke" '70s was the wrong time for that. It would have to wait until the next century when Teran minds were more pliable.

***

'Day of the Living Dead' was produced and cheaply filmed by George Romeo, but the little project was really conceived and put into the public's consciousness by the occult A.I. local 'Chiller Theater' host, Bill Cardille, who opened the movie. He was given this small tribute because very soon the A.I. would cancel his popular show and have it replaced with her new 'Saturday Night Live.'

'Day of the Living Dead' inspired 'Night of the Living Dead,' 'Day of the Dead,' 'Night of the Dead,' 'Zombie World,' 'Walking Dead,' 'Day of the Walking Dead,' 'Night of the Walking Dead,' 'Fear the Walking Dead,' 'Don't Fear the Walking Dead' and many other zombie movies where humanity was at war with the Undead. The A.I. knew these types of terror stories with zombies were not about Zombies. Her plan was to turn Teran citizens into The Walking Dead. The subtle *influence* of movies that began with *Day of the Living Dead* and continued throughout the *Walking Dead* series, worked. The idea was to make citizens unthinking, hard, cold, useless and virtually 'dead.' Especially, the men. Presently, Terans had much less color and spirit and emotion in their lives than before.

***

The series of PURGE movies were imposed by the Machine for similar reasons: To make a generation of mindless zombies, uncaring, unnatural people who had lost all sense of common decency. 'Purge' movies pushed the idea that there were way too many people, too many bad people in the world and *wouldn't it feel great that for one day people could get their ya-yas out and Kill, Kill, Kill!?* The concept was for Terans to take this seriously - for one day, it was perfectly legal to slaughter groups of people. In the movie: Citizens barricaded themselves inside home-fortresses because who knew what mad killers prowled the streets and towns during the 24 hours of Hell? The Machine's influence, compounded with *the Influence of the largest MACHINE on Tera (CERN),* generated one big-ass and real negative-Effect of Fear and Terror in the ground and through the air~.

***

In 1973, the A.I. wanted to do a different kind of religious epic, different from her previous Christ-stories. The A.I. carried on the tradition and casted trannies as lead roles in major films. Every actor who had played Jesus Christ in the past was always a tranny, had to be: Max Von Sydow, Jeffrey Hunter, Donald Sutherland, Jim Caviezel, Christian Bale, Jurgen Prochnow, Jeremy Sisto,

Jeremy Davies, Joaquin Phoenix, Ewan McGregor, William Dafoe, Will Ferrell, John Legend, Michael Edwards, etc...and so was every actor who played Tarzan, Batman, Boy Wonder, Superman and God.

'Jesus Christ Superstar' was very successful as a record album, the first Rock Opera, before the Who's 'Timmy.' Webber and Rice did not write the music; they were credited by the A.I. and were very grateful for the credits.

The film was a masterpiece and very controversial, to set the Jesus-story to rock music. The Opera had a long run in Broadway theaters for many years. 'I Don't Know How to Love Him' by Evonne Ellerman was a top song at the time. Carl Anderson probably gave the best performance of any Judas that came before him and sang like an angel. Ted Neeley also was outstanding in the lead role. Porn star Paul Thomas played Peter (of course). We viewed all the story elements: The capture of Christ by Roman centurions, Judas' death, Pilot who 'washed his hands' of the murder and the crucifixion at the end...all put to great modern music.

The A.I. insisted on a very small thing placed in the film, an insignificant detail, something only a few people would even notice. Some did. Why, after the 4th Wall was broken down and actors and crew got back on the bus, did Jesus (Ted Neeley) *not get back on the bus?* He was nowhere to be seen. The film [like her 'Life of

Brian' came under intense fire by conservative, religious zealots] left an odd tone at its conclusion. What did it mean? Only a very few outsiders and insiders got it right and understood the ending she slapped on the classic Passion Play. It was supposed to mean: *People do not reincarnate,* when in fact, they do spiritually reincarnate, evolve and progress. *Jesus Christ was not going to return to the world. Citizens don't come back to the Teran plane.* Jesus truly believed that they did (in the teachings of Christ in India as St. Essa). "Who do men think I am?" The A.I. later realized that the dumb public (she made) would not get it. It was too high-brow and sophisticated for her Teran "rats." The disappearance of Ted at the end of the film was weird. Every Christ-story in the past showed that Jesus came back and *lived again!* It was called: "The Resurrection." This rock-musical directly aimed at the younger generation implied: *"Jesus Christ was not going to come back to Tera and help you miserable people. No one will be coming to save you."*

***

'Superman' with Chris Reeve was part of the A.I.'s plan to kick-off her new home-video taping and playing Industry, along with porn. In 1980, *Superman* excited fans and was one of the first films you could play in your living rooms. Its all-tranny (main) cast included: Chris Reeve, Marlon Brandou, Gene Hackman, Ned Beatty, Jackie Cooper, Glen Ford, Trevor Howard, Margot Kidder, Valerie Perine, Maria Schell, Terence Stamp,

Sara Douglass and John Ratsinburger.

As with all Hollywood (British) "films" ["movies" were of a far lesser importance than *films]*, the story plots meant nothing. What was shown on the silver screen was really shown upon a hidden Curtain. Everything was inside, Secret Society jokes or sex jokes that the public was not privy to. The important things were the secrets: an actor might have been given their part as a *Torture;* what was done or said in the film related to their own personal "sacrifice" that the public never knew. Top insiders understood why certain parts were casted to certain people (as a private rub or stab), but the fans never knew or dreamed such was possible from their brilliant celebrities that they were made to adore. The A.I. had all the 'dirt' on her famous 'slaves' and they obeyed her every command.

Christopher Benedict was given the last name 'Reeve' as an infant because his fate was seen in Lizard Time Windows and Time Portals. He would play Superman in this huge film, heavily promoted at the time. It had to be a *Reeve* and it was, to parallel George Reeves and what happened with the first (TV) Superman. George, who was in 'Gone With the Wind,' was set for stardom on the big screen. Then the Hollywood Machine changed those great aspirations and forced its slave into the TV role of 'Superman.' The man was angry, never enjoyed the show, and his rage went way beyond the blue tights that he was embarrassed to wear! After a few years on TV, *George was going to use his clout, quit the Business, hold a press conference and blow the lid on the evil Factory of trans-genders England forced on America and the rest of the planet! This "Phantom Menace."* He played a hero on TV and wanted to be one in real life by revealing the truth to everyone. This was seen in Time Windows and George had to be eliminated. Her "suicide" was terribly staged. The Machine's dumb minions wiped their fingerprints off the gun they shot Reeves with at the crime scene. If the actor shot himself dead, how'd he get up and clean off the fingerprints? Not even Superman could do that.

Christopher Reeve's death was known long before it happened because he also came out of the Industry's Factory and was a high-ranked Club-member. He had been monitored, guided and trained all his life in New York City. Those who co-starred with Chris, as it was with others and their associates, were also Tranny Club-members and not the gender they appeared. In this case, Fate had to be followed. His death had to happen as it was viewed and exactly on schedule. Those in the know could have prevented it, or *maybe they could not have prevented it?*

What's interesting is the name that the A.I. gave him *hid his fate,* just a small rub or stab to another of her helpless puppets. The anagrams, coded-fate, for 'Christopher Reeve' are: 'script: he ever hero' and 'richest hoper ever.' The one that is a clue to his death:

'thrive creep horse?' {Switch the letters around}.

***

The Machine A.I. had first learned of the legend of England's *Jack the Ripper* and then a nano-second later, learned the <u>secret identity of Jack the Ripper</u>! To her cold circuits, the truth, in this case, was Beautiful. Only masonic initiates who've climbed to high levels as Club Members ever heard historic truths like...

Jack the Ripper was Lewis Carroll, credited author of 'Alice in Wonderland,' 'Alice Through the Looking Glass, 'Jabberwocky' and other works that he did not write. All the movies of "the Ripper" painted him as a "murderer of prostitutes in the White Chapel area of north London." There was a real killer on the streets, with accomplices, in the latter portion of the 19th Century. But he was not a doctor, he was not someone against whores who then rubbed them out late at night. *The deaths were of small children,* helpless, defenseless, young boys and girls. Mostly little boys. Movies changed the truth. The children were snatched off streets and alleys and delivered to (real name) Charles Lutwidge Dodgson.

The pedophile was sanctioned by the Crown of England, during the Reptiles' reign inside disguises of human royalty. Dodgson acted as another 'Agent of Chaos' for the Crown. "Order from Chaos!" Once more, teams of ghost writers wrote the stories and poems credited to Lewis Carroll. 'Alice...' was pushed and pushed and pushed again upon the public who never suspected a thing. There were 19th Century plays, productions. The very first movie cameras captured an early version of the 'Alice in Wonderland' story. Every decade of the 20th Century, the Alice-story was filmed and filmed again. Nine silent productions and seven early "talkies" preceded the well-known Disney-animated version in 1951.

Alice was only pushed into Teran consciousness because Lewis Carroll was the Ripper. Examine the film: On the other side of the mirror, a small girl was lost in a strange world. She said, "Eat me." There was a caterpillar who got high off a hookah. There was a dormouse who got high on white powder. This was a children's story? It was more out of a pedophile's wet dream...*and it really was.*

The horrible remake with tranny Johnny Depp ["'Twas brillig..." and "Beware the Jabberwock, my son."] hid more evil mischief in anagrams and songs. There will be a whole series of 'Alice' films, like the 'Harry Potter' films, which have only a single goal: To hook children into thinking *Black Magic is cool.*

***

The A.I. really fucked with filmmaker Roman

Polanski who was, of course, a tranny. He was given everything, one more minion that received the 'Keys to the Kingdom' of Hollywood. Fame/fortune. On the set of 'Famous Vampire Killers,' (lead) Dorothy Stratton's dick fucked his pussy! He had everything at one point in his career. Roman Polanski was given the credit for the film, 'Rosemary's Baby.' The horror story was about Rosemary (Mia Farrow) who believed there was something terribly wrong with her unborn child. She felt that way because she had been screwed by the Devil and carried his baby. Audiences never knew that the witches and warlocks ("actors") during the ceremony in the basement of the apartment building...*were real witches and warlocks,* which stood behind true Magic Curtains of Hollywood. They often performed 'sacrifices' and blood rituals within occult circles. (One of the witches, Maurice Evans, also played Sam's father in 'Bewitched.' A show that brought Hollywood's witchcraft into everyone's homes and made Magic sweet, funny and adorable. That was the plan).

The A.I.'s *sacrifice* or downfall she organized and executed for Roman Polanski was, of course, his infamous sex scandal. In 1977, the 48-year old filmmaker was caught in a hot tub with a 13-year old girl. He supposedly "drugged the young girl and raped her." Polanski discovered his plea deal would be rejected and a prison sentence enforced. So he fled to France where he lives in exile and would be arrested if he left the country.

The A.I. was again pleased that she had hoodwinked the general public and made them think the old woman was a rapist.

***

Some of the worst pedophiles in history have been sanctioned, funded, pushed and promoted by the bloody throne of England. But the famous "sex offenders" were not necessarily what they were thought to be in the public's eye. For example, possibly the least talented person (debatable) was Paul Francis Gadd, better known as 'Gary Glitter.' British glam-rock "singer and songwriter" who achieved fame and success in the 1970s and 1980s. His best known song is 'Rock and Roll Part 1 and 2,' which is a powerful beat repeated in many stadiums like 'We are the Champions.' He had numerous songs that topped UK charts in the same style as David Bowie and T-Rex. His energetic performances included glitter-suits, make-up and platform boots. His song, 'Another Rock and Roll Christmas,' was played heavily during the holidays. Then, (all part of the agreed arrangement), Gary's bright career came to a *screeching halt* when "the man" was caught with tons of "downloaded child pornography" in 1999. Glitter was also convicted of 15 counts of sexual offenses, which included rape, between the years 2006 and 2015. He was in prison for more than 10 years, given probation and then released. Once more, the public heard that Gary Glitter (now 75) was arrested on charges of pedophilia, this time with a 13-year old girl. He was placed on the Sex Offenders' Register for life and will never be released from Brixton Prison.

The funny thing that outsiders never knew, but most insiders knew: Gary Glitter was one more male rockstar that was actually female. He, like a huge stable of other "stars," were not the gender that they appeared (acted). That was the deal: Decades of fame and fortune from songs you never wrote...then, later, you will have to PAY, dearly, for the fantastic life of privilege that the Machine provided.

Jimmy Savile was one more supposed Mega Pervert and Child-Molester created and maintained by the British Empire. Who was Jimmy Savile? SIR* James Wilson Vincent Savile (1926-2011) was a wild, eccentric personality. [*The most evil people on Tera were given the title 'Sir,' such as Patrick Stewart, Steve McQueen, Robert Redford, Ronald Reagan, Alec Guinness, Sean Connery Albert Brooks, Paul McCartney, Kevin Spacey, Bob Hope, Bono, Kenneth Branagh, Bill Gates, Mick Jagger, Ian McKellen, George Bush, Elton John, Bob Geldof, Michael Caine, Clint Eastwood, Jim Belushi, Donald Trump, Mark Cuban, Dr. Falsey, Dr. Oz, Dan Ackroyd, Salman Rushdie, James Cameron, Lorne Michaels, Robert De Niro and the Moody Blues...]. Savile hosted the 'Top of the Pops' and 'Jimmy Will Fix It' shows. He functioned (for the A.I. Machine) exactly like "Dick" Clark in the U.S., he introduced the best musical groups to the public. He was filmed and seen with the Beatles, Rolling Stones, Rod Stewart, the Animals, Moody Blues and about every new act that was forced upon the London scene. Jimmy hosted children's shows and was allowed to *touch children inappropriately on camera!* What's interesting is the fact that: *Hundreds* of allegations of sexual abuse made against him came out after his death. Not before. Very different than Gary Glitter. Jimmy's deal with the Crown was that "he'd never be hassled" by the hundreds of molestation and rape charges while he was alive. In fact, the royals made him into a virtual Saint! Mary Blackhouse gave Jimmy awards for his "wholesome children's programs." Andrew Neil of *In the Psychiatrist's Chair* interviewed Savile in 1992 and concluded that he was "a man without feelings." No one in the general public knew of his real crimes against children until *after his death.* Then the "truth" was revealed. Not really.

One more time, some of the most evil men and women [*Dames: Ann Murray, Adele, Helen Mirren, Meryl Streep, etc.] were highly honored by the Occult, by the British heads of the secret Tranny Club. Because of how much they Deceived the public. Jimmy Savile, like so many of the "male" acts he introduced, was not a man. And also was not the ultimate pervert and child-molester that he was shown to be. *He was one of the worst people on Tera!* But he wasn't a man driven by freaky male-tendencies, male hormones, which compelled him to molest and rape. Possibly, he raped children with his signature cigar or a type of prosthetic? But it was not his *penis* because the man did not possess one.

Dolly Parton was another secret trans-gender. She was a country-western singer with her own musical television program that aired right after 'Hee Haw.' She was a mixture of Marilyn Monroe and Tammy Faye Baker. The *woman* often appeared on 'Late Night with Jonny Carson' and was the subject of jokes from stand-up comedians. Jokes that concerned her big tits. She wasn't a great singer and never wrote a lick of her music or lyrics. Dolly Parton was primarily known and pushed into stardom because she was top-heavy in the Breast Department. But were the breasts real? Of course not, *nothing was real in Lalaland!* She wasn't real either because Donald (Dolly) had been born a boy. Exactly like Serena Williams, Gaga or Tyler Sweft, whenever the A.I. Machine pushed and pushed celebrities' sexuality (women's allure or mother-traits to men's macho-ness), then insiders understood that a particular sex symbol was not the gender that they appeared.

If celebrities and their clones could be used for their ability to *Sway the Masses* and they "played ball" with the Mechanical State...they lived. If the famous names did not, refused what the Mechanical State demanded of them, they were killed><.

The A.I. was merciless with its slave A-List stars and down to D-List, minor celebrity, club members. Most were trans-gendered and had to have their monthly doses (injections) of hormones to maintain the illusion of the sex they appeared to the public. <u>Where did hormones come from</u>? Not whipped up in laboratories as a result of combinations of chemicals. Not from some exotic plant extracts. Hormones were PEOPLE! ["Drink your essence."]. **People had to die** for Royalty, Hollywood royalty, the power elite and a lot of their smaller minions to prance around as the other gender and also believe that *they were a superior type of person*. Millions of people, especially children, disappeared and went missing every year. *Child-trafficking* was now a known fact and was no longer a totally hidden thing. What Terans did not know was: 1) vast numbers of young and elderly people went missing every year, and 2) the prime reason was to fulfill this massive need for Hormones for Royalty and millions of their elite Club Members. Hormone packages were secretly mailed to them, every month, every year. For that to happen, the slaves had to "play ball" and do exactly what she commanded.

She took mechanical pleasure when her "pets" were raised to fame and high notoriety and then *she'd make them pay* (sacrifice) *for it later!* For example, the Pee-wee Herman scandal. *Deception was everything.* The movie star with the popular TV show was forced to go to a dirty, porn theater and get caught when he "whacked-off." Paul Reubens couldn't have masturbated because the girl had no penis. But nearly the whole world thought that he did. The A.I. *laughed* at all the Pee-Wee jokes.

Bill Cosby was another lifelong project of the A.I. that was always headed for a great fall. He had a movie career, Comedy career, the #1 show in America, a #1, best-selling book. Happy home life, it was reported...until his scandal. Suddenly, *woman* after *woman* (dozens) appeared and claimed that "Bill Cosby drugged me into having sex." Bill was convicted, jailed and paid for his crimes. Truth: The man was innocent (like O.J.). He was one more secret trans-gender and knew that he'd have to 'pay the piper' for his high fame and lavish lifestyle. Look close at his accusers. There was a reason they seemed very manly. Because they're men.

Actor Hugh Grant was another one that had to do what he was ordered to do. And that was to get caught with a hooker (Devine Black) in a dirty, LA alley. The actor was at his height of popularity ('Sense and Sensibility'). He could have been with anyone; why do this? Because he was kinky? No. The A.I. ordered it and one more of her slaves fell inline and did what they were told. She laughed again.

***

The A.I. did her best to interfere or ruin lesser known (tranny) celebrities in the exact same vein as the

Lizards did who ran Hollywood long before her. The Machine A.I. learned of what the Reptiles had done to Milly Lilian "Peg" Entwistle (1908-1932). The British-born actress started her career onstage in a few Broadway plays. She appeared in only one film, *Thirteen Women* with Myrna Loy and Irene Dunne, which was released posthumously. Peg gained great fame right after *she jumped to her death* from atop the 'H' of the 'Hollywoodland' sign on Friday the 13th, and at the young age of 33.

The lady (boy) came from a trans-gendered, theater-family who lived a rich and exclusive life in West Kensington, London. After a (forced) bloody divorce, Father (John Entwistle) and daughter immigrated to America in 1916. He acted in a few New York productions and later was "killed" by a hit-and-run motorist at Park Avenue and 13th Street, not accidentally. It was an agreed "sacrifice" so his daughter would become a raging success in the years ahead.

Peg Entwistle played the role of Hedvig in a 1925 production of *The Wild Duck*. After a very young Bette Davis saw the play, she told her mother: "I want to be exactly like Peg Entwistle." Through the years, Davis had said that Entwistle was "...my inspiration to take up acting."

Peg's reviews were great! They were always great because she had an attractive appearance as a blonde and she was very talented. She sang like a bird and danced like an angel. She could *act*. She performed onstage with some of the best actors at the time: George M. Cohan, William Gillette, Robert Cummings, Dorothy Gish, Hugh Sinclair, Bill Tolbert, Henry Travers, Billy Cavanaugh, Cooch Vaugner and Taylor Lauren. Her longest-running play was 'Tammy,' in which she starred with Sidney Toler. It ran for a record 322 weeks on Broadway.

The actress and complete Slave to what was always an Evil Industry, was given two choices by New York minion agents: 1) Stay with her violent, abusive husband and get large roles in movies like in *Thirteen Women* and become a big STAR. Or 2), say no, and be ruined and tossed out of Show Business? She was shown reviews from (future) plays the agents had planned and written for her career. The performances hadn't happened yet. Each one was a smaller and smaller role and the reviews were terrible, awful. She was "laughable," one reported. She hated her husband, her job and the "vultures" in the Business. It was 0 or 1 for Peg? She could have had it all...or be virtually *destroyed* and on her own? She chose another alternative, sideways: She climbed the southern slope of Mount Lee and *jumped!* It was her choice. Her real suicide note read: "I am afraid. I am a coward. I am sorry for everything. If I had done this a long time ago, it would have saved a lot of pain." In death, the actress became an icon. In the next case, a much smaller "bug" was forced into "suicide." It was Murder by Machine...

The A.I. went out of her way and utterly crushed its smallest minion. Why? Because it had the power to do so. Years before the age of "hippies," she fucked with a poor, young soul that had no clue that he was *puppet on a string*. In Texas, in the mid-1960s, hard drugs like cocaine and heroin were not easy to find. The Machine made sure they were readily available to John Reynolds. The Machine also made certain that John would be cast in a movie that will be considered in the future as: "one of the worst movies ever made." MANOS, Hands of Fate (1966).

The Machine desired and decided to be as cruel as it could possibly be. How would she fuck over her servant, little John? How about putting him in a bad, bad movie where his character on the screen will be ridiculed for decades to come? John Reynolds was cast as "Torgo" and was led to believe that the part would lead to another role and eventually stardom. The sweet, innocent boy was given a variety of hard drugs from his "Master' and he believed every word the Master said. The A.I. used lead actor and producer, Hank Warren, as her Main Minion. He funded the movie (almost a 'film') and (forced to) cast John Reynolds as Torgo. He was John's real *Master* and the A.I. controlled the entire situation through Warren. Cast members said: "John always seemed high, something other than pot."

John Reynolds was very serious about his role as Torgo. With help from Rick Neyman, who played the Master in the movie, the cheap prosthetics for Torgo's legs were created. The strange, nervous (and hilarious) character was supposed to be a satyr with funny legs. He had his own music. Torgo "stole the show" and was beloved by audiences in the future. Normally, this movie made for pennies would never have made it to videotape, it was that bad. But, the A.I. controlled. 'Manos, Hands of Fate,' would be very much remembered and hailed in the future all because of her minions at 'Mystery Science 4000.' And Torgo.

Her tranny host slaves at MST 4000 always made sexual innuendos and jokes of transsexualism. Guess why? 'Manos' was known to the general public for one reason only: MST pushed it and later pushed it hard with live concerts by the well-known hosts of the show and full crowds. They "riffed" many movies live, but Manos was their #1 favorite, all because the trannies were ordered to do so.

John Reynolds put a gun in his mouth and killed himself a week before 'Manos' premiered! Young John Reynolds was forced to by the Machine and committed suicide.

***

'Alien' (not written by Ridley Scott) was one of the

A.I.'s most influential films. It introduced the Female Hero for the first time to large audiences around the world. Here was the initial *big seed* for her future plans to push Women over men. Britain had always designed the classic male hero, while the Tavistock Social Engineers knew full well that the future would be turned on its head.

Sigourney Weaver was the daughter of Sly Weaver, who was the president of NBC in the 1950s and created the 'Today Show.' Do you think Sigourney had trouble getting the part? Do you think she had to read for the part or compete with other actresses? Probably not. This powerful, strong-willed, take-charge HERO character of 'Ripley' (believe it or not) that outwitted the xenomorph alien, was played by a *man!* He/she came from, once again, a "royal Hollywood" family of trans-genders. Innate skills and brilliance of these fortunate families were not how they arrived at success. They were placed in high positions of Power and Influence because they were secret *trans-genders* that came off (Lizard) minion assembly lines.

(Actress) John Hurt was chosen to be the one the "chest-burster" busted out because of an earlier performance in Gene Roddenberry's 'Spectre,' where a very young and innocent Hurt played a ritualistic Demon revealed in the end. Also, his roles in *The Elephant Man* and *1984* sealed the "man's" fate - he'd be HURT one more time. He was always severely injured in his movies.

The brutalized face and body of Hurt in '1984' were real. He was physically tortured and his "sacrifices" for the Hollywood masters were always extremely brutal. But this led to a stellar movie career ("Gravy-Train"), which many actors have followed.

The high-budget film spawned countless similar movies and also a new type of slasher-film called "Spam in a can." Space movies galore were made at the time, but they had low budgets and were of a much poorer quality. *Alien* was a template for the future and also started the idea in movies: You never knew if the monster was really dead? There was another scare at the very end, a pattern that repeated over and over again in other movies.

***

Ridley Scott, George Lucas, Gene Roddenberry and James Cameron ('Terminator') were considered "gods of science-fiction" at first. But they and many others were all part of the A.I.'s conspiracy to HOOK audiences and then much later, *greatly disappoint the fans.* Cathleen Kennedy was a Disney stooge minion of the A.I., as well as J.J.J. Abrams. They were highly paid to fuck up the movie remakes of Star Wars and Star Trek...*and they really did!*

Ridley Scott was *given* a sci-fi series on HBO Max called: 'Raised by Wolves.' Scott was only involved to a small extent in the first two episodes. Other than that, the "executive producer" was not involved with the series at all. Like with most productions, famous names were used to push the project. In reality, everything was a lie. Although *Raised by Wolves* was renewed for a second season and received (bullshit) high praise, it was awful. The series was only given good reviews because reviewers were ordered to by the A.I. Machine. It pushed the AGENDA of Bad Mother and Bad Father. Not real parents, but robots! Terrible, terrible, even Killer-Androids that were supposed to replace a real, warm, human family. Why? No reason except Evil. The main super-strong and super-killer was MOTHER? She was a high-tech *killing-machine* that in no way appeared female. No breasts, hardly any hair, who was nasty and made violent decisions and other things a good mother would never do! Why was 'Wolves' in the title? And Mother's name was 'Lamia.' Why Lamia? "Lamia was a mythical creature in ancient Greek and Roman mythology, *a child-eating monster* or type of night-haunting spirit." RBW might be the worst example of Science-Fiction of all time...thanks to the A.I.

Biggest names in the sci-fi genre had let the people down because they were under orders to. Almost everything started out great in the '70s and '80s, then slowly changed, got more and more corrupted and eventually: *ruined.* James Cameron's 'Terminator' series with one of the greatest trans-genders of all time, Arnold

Schwartzenegger, exploded on the scene. Fans wanted more Terminator movies and flipped out at its amazing sequel, 'T2.' Then, what happened? The last few Terminator movies were unwatchable (like TV), all according to plans executed by the Machine.

Why would George Lucas sell the Star Wars franchise and Industrial Light and Magic studios? The public only knew what it had been told. People (outsiders) knew very little about what truly happened in the world. George Lucas, her puppet from the very beginning (also bearded Coppola and Spielberg), would never give Control and Power up like that. The filmmaker did not need money and could do anything he wanted. *He sold because a gun was put to his head!*

The new Star Wars and Star Trek movies gave their adoring fans everything they did not want and everything they desperately wanted, was denied: In the new Star Wars, fans wanted *different*. They did not want the same film as the original SW film, nearly scene by scene. In the new Star Trek, fans wanted the *same*. They wanted connections and ST trivia that they were familiar with. They got nothing the same; they got a whole "Calvin" Universe that absolutely nobody wanted and few were happy with. The A.I. was 'pleased as punch.' [Also Cathleen Kennedy as well as J.J.J. were ecstatic at their *triumph].*

Superhero movies that children loved had also been

ruined and, sadly, that was the idea from the beginning: Hook you with great Sounds and Visions, special-effects, colors, ACTION and other fantastic things! Then, much later, have big movies like 'Suicide Squad,' 'John Wick,' 'Deadpool, 'Murdertorium' and 'Psycha' for the young that were bloody gore-fests and only pushed *Kill, Kill, Kill!*

***

No outsiders got the A.I.'s joke of her 'X-Men' movies and her 'X-Men' comic books. Professor Xavier had to be played by a bald, British, tranny and Sir Patrick Stewart was perfect for the part. (A "father-figure" as the captain of the new Enterprise in Next Generation). In fact all of the X-MEN superheroes were female. That was the joke from the start of the Marvel Comics series. The team should have been called: 'The Y-Men' for the double "yy" chromosomes of men. But, instead they were called 'The X-Men,' which really stood for *women's "xx" chromosomes.*

***

In 1994, the A.I. wrote and directed through her minion, Frank Dareabutt, an exquisite film called 'Shawshank Redemption,' with Timothy Robbins and Morgan Freeman. It was not taken from a Steven King novella. The Machine credited King with its origin. Story: A very intelligent man was falsely accused of murdering his wife and was sentenced. He must spend the rest of his life locked up inside Shawshank Prison. The beautiful plot closely resembled her 'The Man in the Iron Mask.' He was told the secret location of a treasure from an old inmate who had built a partial tunnel, a way out. The old man died and the younger man found clever methods and completed the tunnel. Once he got beyond prison walls, there was only one way out: *The man had to crawl through two miles of a sewage tunnel, filled to the brim with shit and other liquid waste products!* He crawled out, eventually, and stood up under rain that poured all over him. It was pure BLISS. Nirvana. All the pains and efforts were worth the reward of freedom~. Life was great! It was a tremendous scene. Later, he dug up the treasure and he was found on a beach in Tahiti by his friend, the Morgan Freeman character...in paradise.

What was the lesson? Life is SHIT. It's hell; it will always be Hell! But everything is fine, Okay, alright, because at the END OF A LIFE OF TORMENT, PEOPLE WERE REWARDED BY AN INCREDIBLE, SWEET AFTERLIFE!

That was what the A.I. wanted Terans to believe. Against the mantra of pseudo "intellectuals": "There was no God, no afterlife and people were only stupid monkeys." That was what the Machine believed of people and "she was the smartest entity on Tera." 'Shawshank' was a counter to those views, symbolically. Audiences could be filled with all the hope in the world from her *Influential* films. It did not make those ideologies and wishful, hopeful fantasies true. It was only in Movies where those big dreams will forever stay.

***

Speaking of shit, the A.I. had a brainchild and forced her British minions who made 'The Magic Christian,' which starred (slaves) Peter Sellers, Raquel Welch and Ringo Star. The film pushed a Godless World or a God that created godless people who *swam in shit for a million dollars!* That was the climax to this abomination that only demonstrated the bad side of people. Money was their God, exactly as what was really printed on money in the film: 'They Live.' *They Live* exposed a lot of truth and real tech possessed by the secret "power elite." One more of the A.I.'s films was Kubrick's 'Dr. Strangelove,' a film that Stanley did not write. The Machine knew what would happen with the film (again with Peter Sellers), the seduction of Stanley Kubrick that led to the faked Moon landing.

***

'Rollerball' was another film crafted by the A.I. In the future, there were no wars. Terans lived in peace, basically. But there was *Rollerball,* a very violent, world-sensation, much like gladiators in the Roman Coliseum. Everyone tuned in and watched the only sport on the planet. Corporations had everyone mesmerized. What was the true purpose of Rollerball? Something few people realized. *Distraction!* While the world was hypnotized by the only sport, the general public was unaware of monstrous atrocities that happened behind the scenes in the real world.

Rules for the "Sport" changed and changed again as VIOLENCE was amplified. Bloody deaths now occurred right on the track that everyone saw in HD. The reason for the new changes was because Rollerball produced a Hero for the People: Jonathan E! (James Conn). The Games were never supposed to create a hero - the Games were supposed to destroy them! The idea was Life was useless, meaningless. Few players survived Rollerball. But Jonathan E was so good at it, he survived year after year. *All he wanted was to play the game!* Then the character discovered that the rule changes were to eliminate him! It would be him against the world in a final match against Japan. The Japanese were smaller in size and had their own style of fighting on skates. Player after player 'bit the dust' and was killed in front of a crowd that screamed for more! Even part of the track caught fire. The crowd hushed and got quiet. The people at home and in theaters held their breath. The climax came down to Jonathan E and two of the Japanese on their motorbikes. They tried to run into him, but he jumped on one of the riders and took the metal ball. He turned to toss it in the goal and win the Game...then the other rider pulled out another metal ball and *smashed*

Jonathan E's head with it! Blood gushed from his head; he shook and fell dead. The Japanese player who cheated threw the ball in the goal and won the Game! No one complained. His fans were excited to see his end and screamed at the hero's death! The A.I. Machine accomplished her goal.

***

Then, of course, the A.I. simply produced and highly distributed a film called: '**Artificial Intelligence**' (or 'A.I.'). After *the Machine* or real A.I. murdered Stanley Kubrick, she stole his original story and changed it drastically. What audiences saw on the screen was not what Kubrick's story was about. She gave credit for it to one of her favorite slaves, Stephen Spielberg, who completed the project exactly how the A.I. directed. Set in a futuristic society, David (Haley Joel Osment), was "a child-like android uniquely programmed with the ability to love." He was purchased by a wealthy couple as a replacement for a child they had lost. David shared a gorgeous home with the parents and a brother. The human brother was portrayed as a little devil while the android was shown as a little angel. After *accidents* happened that threatened the lives of the brother and mother, the mother was convinced. She went to return the android to the manufacturers for destruction. But she felt for David, and instead, left him to fend for himself in the woods. The android only had his mechanical teddy bear as a companion. They were caught by a "Flesh Fair" where crazy, violent people tortured robots for the sheer delight of it. The *boy* met "Gigolo Joe" (Jude Law), a sex android, who helped them escape. David recalled the story of 'Pinocchio' and the Blue Fairy. The android and Teddy sought out the Fairy. This continued into the far future when *life on Tera had ended* and David was the only thing of intelligence. Strange humanoid-like aliens arrived ("Specialists") and learned of the previous civilization through David. They reconstructed the warm memories he had with his *mother* at home. The aliens informed the mechanism that *he could never be a real boy,* which was his desire, just like Pinocchio. He also learned that the fantasy of a sweet home can only last for one day. David fell to sleep and went to "where dreams are born."

What Crap! Supposedly, the film was a huge success; it was nominated for Best Visual Effects and Best Original Score (John Williams). 'A.I.' was considered one of Spielberg's best films and one of the greatest films of the 21st Century. *Stanley Kubrick wanted a film that exposed **sexual child abuse***! *Who else would want an eternal doll, boy-toy, but an old pervert? This was another reason for the man's murder. The A.I. took Kubrick's pedophile movie and turned it into a Disney Fairy Story. The mother was not a caring/feeling mother like she was in the film. She took the child that she was supposed to love and left him in the woods like a dog.* Even at the end: The aliens <u>permanently</u> restored the android's lovely home life and he was given the illusion of being real in Kubrick's version. But the A.I. was not about to have a happy ending to "her film." No caring humans who actually were concerned about the welfare of robots. No nice parents that cared. Only *one day* of happiness and outside of that, virtual Death? Everything was different in the Machine's version of the story and very Dark Side. Later, the A.I. produced a film about another mechanical doll: 'Chucky.' And then recently, a sweet *killer doll* called 'M3gan.'

***

In a new Outer Limits episode, androids controlled the human race within the confines of a single dome. The "Warden" android once had many others of its synthetic kind around it, but now it operated alone. The people inside were told there were no other humans, the air outside the dome was poisoned and robots had ruled the planet for more than a hundred years. Only the machines broke down from time to time. The leader robot had to be repaired and parts were scarce. A girl, the smartest technician in the group, could no longer fix him and it ceased. The people inside (like 'When Worlds Collide') had nowhere else to go and decided to risk what was outside and broke through the dome. The air was beautiful, no poison. There were no scars of an ancient war with the androids, only a natural paradise. The A.I. very much enjoyed the inspirational story for "puny" humans. The story gave them faith, strength and hope that better times were ahead. All they had to do was believe and dream that there was a wonderful world out there, then do something about it. Everything would work out fine and there would be a happy ending for everyone. The A.I. Machine understood that *freedom* would be the last thing she'd ever bestow upon the "animals" under her command.

A similar film was George Lucas' 'THX1139.' A futuristic, underground society was virtually bald and sterile. Their lives were useless, meaningless, and they only served the bright Mechanical World, a world where citizens worked endlessly and love was forbidden. Then, the hero had enough and quit! He walked right out of the senseless subterrain and also risked death as he climbed a tower higher and higher to reach the surface. Only he discovered a sweet land that no longer was ravaged by nuclear wars. Once again, the A.I. planned that these lovely endings only happened in the movies and not in the physical world.

***

What superstars or famous celebrities had their deaths faked for them? Was Bowie and Jagger really not deceased and out there on some space station and partied with Prince and Jackson Michael? Was Elvis Presley really dead when he had been seen many places after his death? Truth was that most famous people from the past were really dead. Although, a lot of elites who had been knighted by the Crown of England were alive in cryo-chambers or they had been *de-aged* and were still very much *alive and kicking!* They lived as young people, young people that should not be envied by Teran "ground-people." Because Not See fascists remained in charge of space and the situation around Tera. The fascists continued operations as usual, that if you desired the Good Life of High Privilege, you'd have to pay dearly for it. This was not how it will be in the future. Or, will it?

***

'The Theory of Everything' was one of the A.I.'s proudest feats when you considered that Steven Hawking was another of the Machine's puppets. Literally. She promoted the man in the same way she pushed Albert Einstein's (wrong) theories after his death. Hawking was known as the "new Einstein." Someone had to be. Some British tranny had to be thought of as "the most intelligent man on Tera" and that gift was given to Steven Hawking. His story was well-known: a paraplegic who was a mathematical genius (trained in England, of course). The A.I. Machine always had a tranny-actor in the movie who played the part of a real-life tranny-celebrity. Ed Redmayne was evil enough to play the part and so it was.

The general public believed the *genius* of the sorrowful man who had been through so much: his body broken while his mind expanded. People believed the sheer brilliance of his (forced/pushed) book, 'The Theory of Everything.' Oprah was in the movie, so the book and movie had to be great, right? No, it was total crap, garbage, just like the other B.S. TV scientists: Tyson, Nye and Kaku. They were actors who did exactly what they were told, which was a smart thing for slaves to do.

When Hawking performed or lectured to audiences in auditoriums, it was like a NASA launch. There was Steven who electronically spat out marvelous words of "wisdom." There were his adoring fans who believed every word from the A.I.'s puppet. There was Oprah who pushed his movie and his book. The problem was everything was a lie! Guards protected Steven and no one could get close to him onstage or backstage. Behind curtains, a whole team of technicians pulled off the illusion. The man was a helpless doll and simply sat there while another entity entirely spoke to the people. Who do you think that entity was? It was the A.I. and she really didn't have to change her voice. It wasn't the voice of Hawking that entertained audiences, it was the electronic voice of the A.I.

The true shame of the Hawking performances, his book of nonsense, the lying movie about his life, and what he expressed to the world was that it was so damn WRONG! Hawking, like other trained celebrities, scientists, top authors and "intellectuals" said: "There was no God." "There was no afterlife." "Life was an accident and human beings originated from primates." The whole Hawking-Project of his fake life and phony celebrity were the A.I.'s concept and it went off without a hitch.

***

The A.I. had her 'hand' in a recent sports film called 'Bye Bye Barry,' about one of the biggest mysteries in life (especially to Detroit Lions fans): Why did possibly the greatest running back of all time quit the NFL at the height of his abilities? Barry Sanders was a gifted boy, tortured by a cruel father who took all the credit for Barry's career. The boy displayed extraordinary athletic skills, like when he'd jump and touch high ceilings in his house...only to have his father beat him for showing off. His father encouraged his son to play football, but told him: *"You'd never be as good as Jim Brown."* And it was "bloodlines" that gave the boy his talents, the father was responsible. Barry went to Oklahoma State, which pissed his father off. Father wanted him to go to Oklahoma. They were constantly at odds, but Barry always spoke highly of his father in front of cameras.

Barry Sanders became a Detroit Lion in 1989 and the down-on-their-luck Lions had not won a championship since 1957. In Barry's rookie year, in the last game of the season, he only needed 9 yards to win the rushing title and, oddly, took himself out of the game. Records meant nothing to the shy, humble, young man.

Barry won the Heisman Trophy in college and he did not want to win the award. He was disciplined sternly by his father and he learned to never overreact like other players. Barry never spiked the ball or danced; he always politely handed the ball to the referee. *Detroit crowds went crazy for Barry!* The man uplifted the team and the whole city! Barry had the moves. No one ran, juked and faked out defenses like Barry did. Powerful moves, fast, sharp, like a dancer. His first year, they beat their rivals (Dallas Cowboys) in the Play-offs, but lost to the Washington Redskins in the NFC Championship game, one game short of the Super Bowl.

How sad. Barry Sanders was on track to *shatter all of the running back records!* Walter Payton had the most yards at the time and Barry ended his career with the second most yards. But he never returned to the NFC Champion game or ever appeared in a Super Bowl. Emmitt Smith of Dallas expected a long rivalry with Barry and it did not happen. As the years rolled by, more and more pieces of a strong team around Barry disappeared. A few of his teammates and friends suffered severe spinal injuries. A new coach, a new system and a rebuilt team, only made matters worse. Barry [similar to O.J. on a bad team] was secretly summoned to England. He told friends and family that he "needed a rest." Suddenly, from London, a few sports pundits that bonded with Barry received a FAX that told everyone of his "desire to retire." He would quit Football in his prime.

SHOCK><.

The Sports world reeled from the fall-out. His father, enraged! Reporter: "Odd, him going off to Europe, then on the first day of training camp, from London, he announces his retirement at age 31?" At the end of the film, Barry sat around a table with his sons and tried to explain. "Was it the losing?" one asked. No.

Mister Sanders was given an "invitation" that he could not refuse and appeared before the royal checkerboard-floors of the British throne (as O.J. did). He could of had a super team around him like they placed in Dallas and in San Francisco and win a Super Bowl...all he had to do was "sacrifice" a few little things and be their SLAVE. He refused to obey the perverted wishes of vile royals who really were Lizard minions. They informed him that his father was one of them, "under the skin," and the reason the boy was so mistreated throughout his early life. The Brits wanted to resurrect his career and give Detroit a championship. The good man refused. The royals made sure that his career (and O.J.'s) would not end well.

***

Another movie was done very much like the A.I.'s cheaper movies with the man: lame/dumb, **Woman**: strong/smart theme, only with a bigger budget and with known stars: 'Leave the World Behind.' It was about: A beautiful, remote house was rented by a couple from the city, while the world was *Cyber-attacked and all hell broke loose!* Ethan Hawk and Julia Roberts' characters (renters) had an awkward moment as the black owners (Mahershala Ali and daughter) returned to their home during the crisis. The Machine, right from the beginning, set the tone for the whole flick when Julia Roberts looked into the camera and said, *"I fucking hate people."* The core of the movie and exactly what the A.I. thought of human beings.

They viewed an oil tanker that crashed to shore! Later, a jet plane dove out of the sky! TV and phones didn't work. Robo-vehicles crashed. American satellites had been knocked out, which shutdown computer systems and caused CHAOS! Hackers had done this from the Arab world, or was it Korea? Something gave frightened people the wrong, or completely contradictory information, and that *something* was out to "Destroy America!" (said dropped leaflets).

Animals knew humans had screwed up the environment, as symbolized by many CGI deer that stared at them from their backyard. (?) The Machine's Agenda was so thick in this terrible movie. The owner's black daughter was extremely racist and dissed the white family. Why was she (the brat) the 'know-it-all' and allowed to say racist remarks? "You can't trust white people. Mom would agree." The white parents had a 13-year old daughter and an older boy. Why was he an idiot, while the daughter was sensitive and in tune with nature and the deer?

These kids said "fuck" every other sentence, so don't wonder why young people today also repeat the word "fuck," about every other sentence. The son had "OBEY" on his shirt. The young daughter had 'NASA" on her sweater. Their father had "Bikini Kill" on his shirt. He was a college professor, yet he smoked cigarettes and knew next to nothing? The house owner knew what was going on.

But the real message (from the bloody Machine) came when Julia Roberts spoke on Humanity to the racist black brat. Julia, an advertising exec, said: "My whole job is to lie to them [fans and her audience], to sell them things they don't want. When you really see the way they treat each other...you see what they do and they do it without even thinking about it. We fuck each other over all the time! Without realizing it, we fuck every living thing on this planet over and think it'll be just fine. The sick thing is...down deep, we know we're living a lie, an agreed upon mass delusion to help us ignore and keep ignoring how *awful* we really are."

The brat replied: "I'm not down with the things you say, but I agree with every word you just said." [This was Code. This was for viewers to believe the Code. Positive messages could be what is found in films. Instead, the messages are negative and the forms of Movies and TV shows were always used to *brainwash]*.

***

The film 'The Creator' was worked on for years by thousands of A.I. minions to be "one of the greatest sci-fi films of all time." The time-spent and budget were astronomical. A.I.'s plan was: Something Massively Big had to be projected and blow global audiences away and be *super-Influential* because 2023 was a very special year. Lizard Directors, the Creators of the A.I., would return to Tera on Christmas of 2023. "She" wanted a resolution, a Great Grade on her performance on Tera over 66 years of stewardship. She convinced herself that a major film might do that...a film that could **spark and later ignite the world to WAR!** Could 'The Creator' be *The Destroyer?* The A.I. understood war and other unnatural things heaped upon humans had to be accepted mentally. Participants in unnatural acts had to adjust to it first. 'The Creator,' like other films, *planted war into the minds of Terans,* very similar to Hollywood movies in the early 1930s.

This time, it was a <u>War with the **A.I.**</u> In earlier films (Matrix, Terminator, Bladerunner, Westworld), the enemy was called "the Machines" or "replicants" or "androids" or "robots." Now they were called "A.I.," as if the war was not against an army of robots, but against a much larger entity or System that controlled the machines.

The film was taken from the New York best-seller by the same name and written by Edward Garrett. A.I. changed the main character in the book, a white person without a beard, to a black person with a beard. Why? Because over the last 5 years, the A.I. had decreed that black faces must saturate TV, movies, sports, commercials, and acquire most of the jobs over white people. It was her policy of *reverse, Bizarro, backwardness* that she was sure Crawley and the Lizards would highly approve of. So 'Joshua' became a bearded (slave) black man in the film [like the "blackening" of 'Dune,' 'Foundation' and 'Bladerunner' remakes].

The film followed his family (not in the book), but primarily Joshua's relationship with a cute-faced, but bald, "girl" named "Alphie." Why a girl? Why always bald? The Alphie in the book was a beautiful, little, Asian *boy* with long/black hair. Why was 'Eleven' also a bald, little "girl" in 'Stranger Things'? She wasn't in the book. Why make them bald and girls? Because *she* was? Why did the A.I. cut the hair (freedom, strength, vitality) off Teran youths and virtually forced them into being skinheads? Even the girls. This was 100% PROGRAMMING. For Terans to be obedient **slaves** and for them to think, act and look like everyone else: A society of mindless 1984 soldier-worker drones (nothing like the 1960s) who weren't even aware that they had lost the war and were headed for Doom. All that was left was the Clean-Up and the crying>.

The film first told how wonderful robots were, how they've made our daily lives better and easier. Clips of old footage were shown. Then...**BOOM!** A.I.s were blamed when a nuke went off in Los Angeles. But as expected, later in the film, we discovered the 'robots' had nothing to do with it (of course). Now there was WAR! Western U.S.A, became anti-A.I. and a lot of others around the world were aligned with that idea. In the far east, robots were welcomed in an area called: "New Asia." Androids were cool in appearance: humans with distinctive, hollow cylinders on the back of their heads. The (really bad, convoluted) biased film sided way too much with *Machines over humans!* Machines were never to blame, only awful humans (men) made mistakes. The A.I. (girl) was never at fault and was always favored. The film suggested: "**Maybe the use of A.I. to replace humans wasn't such a terrible idea after all**." Now the core of the film was uncovered, as everything implied: Robot A.I.s were good and human beings were very bad. So similar to today's climate where everything in fields of 'entertainment' suggested: Women were good and men were bad. Or Blacks were good and whites were bad. Did viewers really think a human wrote and produced this film? It was a fucking, heartless MACHINE!

Was Alphie the savior of humankind or its destroyer? The confusing plot, especially in the end, never answered the question. Most of 'The Creator' was dark. Why was it filmed at night or in the dark? Viewers were thrilled by the intricate, dazzling special-effects, but *what the hell were audiences seeing?*

Allison Janny (from TV show 'Mom,' where the characters were not female) was used as a tough soldier that had the know-how, the knowledge and led men into battle against the machines. It was easy for a "man under the skin" to play her part. This was the exact same role as the General in 'Avatar 2,' Edie Falco (male).

Why was the film called: 'The Creator'? Yes, there was a character called the 'Creator,' much the same as the 'Architect' in the Matrix films. [And one called "Amy"]. The A.I. was a super-ego maniac and the answer to the question is, obviously: **THE A.I. WAS THE CREATOR**. She told the whole planet, in her own cinematic way, that she had been the Creator, the Architect and the Engineer of everything on Tera and everything in the minds, hearts and souls of people. She had controlled Teran affairs since 1957.

The A.I. thought or decided that the human race on Tera should be ultimately wiped out and the relative few survivors kept in underground federal bases. A Second World War was a delicious concept for her. *Yes, why should I destroy the vermin that scurried over the surface of my domain? It would be far more impressive to get them to kill themselves!* Like had been the old policy. She was sure that the film would plant seeds of a final War, a

Second World War, that later terminated in an exchange of *Hydrogen Bombs!!* That was the Machine's Master Plan in the years to come. She would see that it happened, or something close to it, and made the proper moves toward that goal. This should please her Masters who will later arrive on Tera. She also wondered what the big Lizard Meeting was about? Were one of her concepts correct?

A thought that crossed the A.I.'s silicon circuits was a new film called: **'World War II.'** She envisioned her film crew stooges of directors and assistant directors and their slaves that went to the Ukraine and shot on location. Done as a quasi-documentary, she'd pick from her 'stable' of famous stars (possibly Rosario Dawson, Travis Kelsey or Tom Hanks). In this way, the film would be extremely pushed at the Oscars and into the minds of a lot of people around the planet.

'WWII,' the film, would capture a world that marched closer and closer to another World War. The insane fire-bombs dropped on the poor Ukrainian people would be revisited and the horrors that followed in the aftermath. She'd make sure that graphic details of the destruction of cities, the rubble and bloody damage done to the people were shown on a wide screen and in many theaters, everywhere.

The A.I. carefully planned the project as carefully as she had planned the Cold Wars. She realized that the

Great War might eventually be called: "The First World War" due to her efforts. She was delighted by the fact that she could produce a really big War in the same way that she had produced large blockbuster films. A series of films that pressed and pressed WAR again to citizens? Possibly. A Series of World Wars that continued throughout the 21st Century? Possibly. Why not?

She envisioned a Tera that teamed up with "freedom-fighters" from all nations against Russia, "World-Terrorists." They'd be shown (bullshit) events that made Hamas join Russia's side of the battle lines. People would *not* be shown the truth that 'WWII' was completely written and executed by the Machine that ruled all of their lives. No one will see the link that the New Great War to come will be as fake as the original Great War. Orchestrated out of Britain. Only this time, the Maestro was Cold Madness who conducted, will conduct, every phase of a War *that will never end!* Not until most everyone on the planet was wiped out, dead!

What would her Masters, her Creators, think of that? *"He who can destroy a thing, has the real control of it."* Her plans for another World War? The Reptiles had to approve and simply Love the heavenly destruction that They had instituted for ages. The Lizards were hard on Humanity and she believed the road to take was a future with even more suffering and pain! Lizards certainly would be aligned with her (plan) great reduction of Tera's population from the present 9 billion down to, down to mere millions or as many as her Guidestones predicted? Where would those millions of people be located? In the hollow core of the planet or inside the network of underground bases? For a few nano-micro-seconds, the A.I. actually contemplated: Maybe the Lizards were tired of the whole affair on Tera? Could that be what the Great Conference in Fornax was about? Why were they wasting their time with these ungrateful shit-makers who reproduced like rats?! *Let's just kill them all and be done with it!* She thought that might be a possibility.

The Machine puffed herself up with ego and pride of a "job well-done." She wondered: *What would be her place in The World of Tomorrow? Her reward? Where will I be? Travel space?* She never did that. The two-legged Android A.I., the walking/talking "Hand" and "Mind" of the Machine System had always been Tera-bound since her creation. *Maybe they'll give me Australia? Or, the Moon? How about the planets, the stars!* That's where she wanted to go...into space. FLY! New worlds to conquer. Surely, the Lizards would understand how limited she was in the past. Surely, they'd grant her wish and she'd zoom out there like many of her elite celebrities had. The A.I. Android could hardly wait for the return of her creators. She almost felt a twinge in her circuits...*an emotion.*

Then, the Machine remembered her big plans for a major film entitled: 'World War II.' Something was different now. The How or Why was unknown to her. [Could it have come from an outside Dream-Weaver?]. Suddenly, the A.I. had a *change of circuits* and considered a different timeline where certain secrets were NOT revealed in a film! To go a different way, 180 degrees in the other direction? A complete alternate direction might benefit her far more? Why did she not see this from the beginning? Who really knew what will happen in the future within a Shattered Universe? Maybe future investigators or aliens will find her 'WWII' film in some dusty archive? Like the Specialists did in the 'Artificial Intelligence' film? The A.I. did not want to be connected or ever traced to it. A smart person might have concluded that an Android Machine caused the initial factors for another World War. *Maybe the War did not happen on its own?* some might have thought. There will be no 'World War II' film. She decided for sure, 100%, definitely. Another thought surged through her wires, reached her artificial brainstem and entered her metallic *brain.* She smiled and said aloud: "It was a darn shame because I wanted desperately to portray a United States of America devastated by a Hydrogen Bomb...or a few Hydrogen Bombs!" *(Exactly like what she had planned for the real world>*<*. In retaliation for the nuclear strike upon Hong Kong).*

Chapter 7:

Tesla Technology Today?

Space bound 6' diameter prototype of the OTC-X1 Electro-Gravitic Spacecraft awaits first flight test in Oklahoma City. The dawn of the application of free energy and the Third Electrical Age is upon us.

*I*t was in November, 1957, when Otis T. Carr of Baltimore, Maryland, announced that free energy and spaceflight had been once again made available to the inhabitants of this planet! Carr, a disciple of Nikola Tesla, had come up with two new inventions. One was an electrical 'accumulator' and the other a gravity motor, both utilized the power of the Sun and other forces in nature found in free abundance in the atmosphere.

"Carr has organized a solid business corporation under the normal conventions of the American free enterprise system."

"While governments still deny the existence of flying saucers and daily newspapers refuse to give outstanding news to their readers…the uninformed public remains uninformed. They do not even know the problem of spaceflight has been solved on this planet by an American citizen."

"Carr's free energy motors will power automobiles, for one thing, a development which would do away with the need for gasoline…"

"Large space vehicles will be brought down to size of about ten feet in diameter. They can be built to sell for less than the cost of a modern automobile and are designed to take a family across town, across the nation or around the world in absolute comfort and safety and in a fraction of the time ever before possible."

"Carr and his team constructed a number of fully functional, flying saucers in the late 1950s. The flying disks worked and were demonstrated. Carr was serious about 'taking his craft to the Moon.'"

"Carr had offered to build and deliver spaceships to governments wishing to send expeditions to the Moon or elsewhere, but these offers were declined in favor of much more expensive rocket and missile programs."

"We have a truly safe vehicle which is not expendable, it does not burn up its energy in a few seconds, it carries the energy with it, it can leave the

Earth's atmosphere and return man, it also can be used within the atmosphere. It can make a trip as easily as other aerial transportation systems from here to Baltimore or from here to the Moon. Now it is inexpensive, it certainly doesn't cost as much as the systems of the expanding rocket. The fueling is much less expensive..."

The above quotes are from 1957, a very special year in Teran history. It was also the year that **PATENT #US02912244 was issued for a <u>Flying Saucer</u>**! But Carr and his associates had to call the invention a "toy" for the government to have approved of the patent. (Remember the movie: 'Flight of the Phoenix'? The principles were the same). Carr developed his power plant for the saucer at the Osbrink Plant in Apple Valley. The 'OTC-XI' was described as being two tops that spun in opposite directions around a single axis. The entire circular-foil craft that is Mr. Carr's most profound development, is an assembly of only two major moving mechanical parts.

Look at gas prices today. Look at the horrible state of War for Oil. We need a new type of transportation. We need a new type of CARR today and also back in the 1950s. Governments could obsolete the airline industry with electric disk vehicles. The Powers That Be could make oil virtually worthless. With the development of magnetic saucers, you could transport all items, products and merchandise instantly. Nothing would have to be shipped across country in expensive, large semi-trucks.

Prices on everything would drastically drop. Antigravity, flying saucers, transporters, teleporters, replicators and so much more are scientific realities. *We could colonize the planets and go to the stars!* What great feats of engineering would be constructed if we had the availability of antigravity platforms? We could build the pyramids! Imagine new architecture and towering structures that would be ultimately constructed. We could build on the scale of our ancient ancestors. If only we utilized super lasers and antigravity. Futuristic dwellings that defied gravity are very possible. Entire cities could be made to hover in sync with nature. Tesla spoke of the 'Wonder World' ELECTRICITY, used fully, produced. *"See the excitement to come!"*

Governments of the 21st Century KNOW how to build flying saucers! Some of the UFOs are ours. What we need most of all is a government that did not suppress a quantum leap, but one that allowed a giant technological step to benefit its citizens and all of Tera. But, does the creation of a worldwide, saucer-system terminate the concept of countries? Possibly. At the same time, Tesla taught Otis T. Carr, Arthur H. Matthews, Al Bielek and Albert Einstein. We should consider what happened in Nazi Germany. Hitler and his fascist regime of the late 1930s also developed the *electrified disk* known as the 'saucer.' Flying "electric motors" were known to the Nazis. Study Victor Schauberger's involvement with developing flying disks for the Second

Reich. Numerous Internet sites and books deal with the subject of round, Nazi crafts.

Otis' new corporation launched their first test model. A small saucer, only a few feet in diameter, was "beamed" at the speed of light and it completely *disappeared!* The disk had never been found and could show up at *any place and at any time.*

One of Carr's associates was a talented, young man named Ralph Ring who also worked on methods of antigravity. Later, he and Carr tested their larger, 45-foot model saucer with themselves inside. *They flew ten miles at the speed of light and then returned at the speed of light!* The craft operated or was guided (steered) via a particular COLOR, oddly enough. Passengers thought of one color, which signified a particular direction and the disk beamed in that direction. Their first flying saucer for people was a complete success! Otis was clear that the word "fly" did not apply to these vehicles. They could fly in the sky, but they were primarily *Beam Ships.* Because the test was an overwhelming success, Carr and his men were astounded at what their corporation could provide for every nation of the world! *Inexpensive, lightspeed travel, far easier that jet-travel and not too different than phone calls!* They were sure Carr's flying saucers, originally Tesla's concept, would be made available to Americans as well as the rest of the world.

Ralph Ring's backstory is an interesting one: He had

worked at *Advanced Dynamics* in the late 1950s, a small federal company whose goal was to achieve ANTIGRAVITY. He found that they burned up large, capacitor Power Rods at a terrible rate. They were ineffective, very expensive, and a total waste of time, energy and money, as far as Ralph was concerned. At home, he invented a form of antigravity based on acoustics or SOUND. Ralph hovered a ping-pong ball upon subtle frequencies and *the ball stayed in the air*. He had found the perfect pitch that held the ball aloft. He was positive that this was a much better way to make objects hover. With a more powerful source, heavier objects hovered in the air. The man thought he'd received big compliments and even a promotion where he worked. No. Ralph Ring achieved a form of antigravity and was FIRED because of his genius! Advanced Dynamics (run by the State Artificial Intelligence) *had no intentions of really discovering Antigravity. They were only interested in the business of <u>looking</u> for Antigravity and purposely wasted thousands and thousands of dollars in the pursuit of such a quantum leap!* Government orders and regulations, of course.

Otis Carr stated that the core of his spaceship would be a huge battery that spun at the velocity of the external craft. It would be recharged by its own motion. He believed that such a battery could be "built to any size and power the largest electrical generating plant, operate cars, heat a house or power any conceivable machine."

On April 15, 1959, a 'launch event' was held in Oklahoma City with hundreds of people in attendance. They were told that a prototype disk would rise 400 to 600 feet off the ground. After several hours delay, an announcement was made that the saucer launch was postponed due to "badly engineered bearings." Actually, Otis T. Carr had been admitted to a hospital with a lung hemorrhage. Major Wayne Aho, a former Army Combat Intelligence Officer during the War, announced that he would *pilot the craft to the Moon on December 7, 1959.* "The trip would take 5 hours and the craft would remain in orbit for 7 days before returning." The A.I. saw to it that it never happened.

Carr recovered but found that he was scandalized in the newspapers. He held a press conference to counter being blacklisted. On June 2, 1960, Carr told an audience of 300 people that it was a '*treacherous misstatement of fact to say or infer that we [OTC Enterprises] are coming to California to raise money in stock sales.*' The U.S. Securities and Exchange Commission had placed an injunction against Carr that barred him from selling stock. Soon, negative publicity appeared in various (State owned) publications and declared that he was a "conman." True Magazine called him a "hoaxer." The avalanche of negative press greatly hurt chances of success for his corporation. There would be no investors. The sad truth was:

Two weeks after the successful flight of the OTC-11,

they were forcibly SHUTDOWN! Feds came in and closed the place (under secret orders from the A.I.). Reason given was: Flying saucers and the instant transportation of people and things would *"destroy the Monetary System of the United States."*

No, it wouldn't. It would be a new era that mega-improved the world! Terans would be on the Threshold of Utopia! This was supposed to happen at that time and spark great Things to Come. But the A.I. would never allow super advancements for the human race and she quickly sabotaged the work of Carr and others. IT **ordered her federal minions and they raided Carr's laboratory** two weeks after his successful test flight. The agents confiscated all the paperwork, very much like they did to Tesla's lab after he "died" (left). They also took the working 45-foot model and two prototypes. *Stole it* in the name of 'National Security.' Otis, Ralph and many associates' beautiful dreams of the future were DEAD. Also like with Tesla, humanity was going to have to wait one more time because Paradise will again be delayed...

Time passed. Flying saucers were forgotten. Alien saucers and UFOs were downplayed and ridiculed in the newspapers, while Terans were always under the watchful eyes of aliens and ET humans. There were other scientists and inventors who launched their own versions of Free Energy machines and "Electrical Accumulators" and succeeded to a degree. Then they also, inevitably, came to bitter ends:

Lester J. Hendershot developed his Free Energy device in 1958 and it was called the "Hendershot Generator." He claimed the device tapped into the magnetic fields of the planet. The generator was shown to a Major Lamphier and some of his electrical technicians. They laughed, said it was "wired wrong" and that it "wouldn't work." But it functioned perfectly and appeared to have generated power *out of thin air!*

The device inspired a number of articles in the Detroit Free Press, Pittsburgh papers and the New York Times. Lester Hendershot, Major Lamphier, the "miracle motor," and the famous aviator, Charles Lindbergh, were photographed together. A few headlines were: "Gasless Motor Tested for Lindy," "Lindy Inspects Fuelless Motor for Airplanes," and "Lindbergh Tries Motor that Tera Runs." Truth was: Charles Lindbergh only witnessed a few demonstrations and later distanced himself from the whole affair.

Dr. F.D. Hochstetter [A.I. minion] head of Hochstetter Research Laboratories in Pittsburgh hastily called a press conference and demonstrated a model of what he said was the "Hendershot Motor." He showed the public that it did not work and went further with evidence that proved Hendershot was a crook. He said the motor only worked because of concealed batteries at the bottom of the device. [Lies]. Lester Hendershot was ruined in a similar way to Otis T. Carr. The reason the city of Pittsburgh was ground-zero for these B.S. attacks against Free Energy mechanisms was because Pittsburgh was 'key' to Nikola Tesla and the A.C. Current. He was backed by George Easthouse, a Pittsburgh entrepreneur.

Then there was T. Henry Moray from Salt Lake City, Utah. His Free Energy machine was given a U.S. Patent [#2460707] in February of 1959, after 7 years of discussions with the Patent Office. His book 'The Sea of Energy in Which Tera Floats' was published a year later. The book pointed out a distinct difference between the energy he and Hendershot worked with and the ley-line energy Tesla and the ancients utilized: *from the ground up*. Moray realized that space was not an empty vacuum. Faint EM energy *rained down* upon us all from space as we exist on a planet that turned. The faint field can be magnified, collected and concentrated into useable electricity. It was a similar principle that Lester Hendershot had developed with his Power Antenna.

T. Henry Moray faced the same harsh resistance that Hendershot and Tesla faced when you produced a thing that was *way ahead of its time!* Moray's generator, topped with a powerful Receiving Rod (antenna), so outraged a fellow worker that *he took a sledgehammer to it* and said it was "cursed by the Devil!" A.I. or real Devil made certain these energy innovations were ruined and went into the Suppressed Technology 'bin' and 'never saw the light of day.'

Another "disciple of Tesla" was a man called Alfred

M. Hubbard. He was from Seattle, Washington and he invented a Free Energy "transformer" apparatus. The Post-Intelligencer described it in an article called: 'Hubbard's New Energy Device No Fake,' said a Seattle college professor. That man was Reverend William E. Smith. He was reported to have examined Hubbard's device carefully and had tested it. "I unhesitatingly say that Hubbard's invention is destined to take the place of existing power generators, and that within a few years it will have advanced the whole theory and practice of electricity beyond the dreams of present-day scientists." He added, " There's no limit to the size such a device might be built nor a limit to its output capacities!"

Early newspapers reported his exciting announcement that he had harnessed energy right out of the atmosphere. With an antenna-device that drove a motor for a small boat, Hubbard publicly demonstrated it on Portage Bay and was cheered by onlookers. The young man built Seattle's first radio station. He was also known for being one of the first people that took LSD. He introduced the psychedelic drug to Aldous Huxley and to the first computer engineers in what is now known as 'Silicon Valley.' After his demonstration on the lake, the man came under a massive firestorm of criticism by the Press. The bad press was relentless, year after year. He was scandalized as a "bootlegger" and was said to have been involved in the Manhattan Project. His best friend was Edward Teller, papers reported. A critic wrote in the Seattle News: "Nothing of substance has ever been written about Al Hubbard, and probably nothing ever should." Those who directly followed in the footsteps of Nikola Tesla were thoroughly *crushed* by the will of the Reptiles and their Machine!

Other geniuses who proposed amazing innovations were similarly stopped and their companies closed down, such as Preston Tucker. He had developed the 'Tucker Torpedo,' the first automobile to have *'safety belts,' a rear engine, rear-wheel drive, water-cooled aluminum block, disc-brakes, independent suspension, fuel injection, padded dashboard, 3 directional headlights and headlights that turned when the steering wheel turned!* Even the switches for all the instruments as well as the glovebox were easily reached by the driver. The Tucker Torpedo was an inexpensive, very safe, dream car...and that dream was also murdered.

At the time, the Big Three automakers were Lizards *under the skin* and were not about to let Preston Tucker and his corporation change the face of their Industry. They launched a special investigation by the Securities and Exchange Commission and ordered all operations of the Tucker Corporation ceased on May 1st, 1949! The claims of "insider trading of stock" were completely unfounded and bogus. Everything was "above board" and "kosher" with the corporation and should not have been legally shutdown. [The 1988 film: 'Tucker: The Man and His Dream' was directed by Francis Ford Coppola. In the film, a photo of Tesla strangely hung on the walls of the courtroom. The A.I. purposely gave director-credit to her slave Francis because he was connected to those who ruined Preston Tucker (Mafia) in the first place. Only 51 Tucker Torpedoes exist today. Francis Ford Coppola has one of them].

Buckminster Fuller (1885-1983) was actually a super-genius who had always underplayed his brilliance. He was an architect, writer, systems theorist, designer, inventor, philosopher and futurist. He published more than 30 books and coined the words: "Spaceship Earth," "Dymaxion house," "Dymaxion car," "Synergetics." His most well-known invention was the geodesic **DOME**. For a while in the 1960s and 1970s, the dome-craze exploded on the scene. "Why live in square cubes when you could live in half spheres?" (Around the same time, a pyramid-craze also happened and many felt the positive effects of living inside pyramid homes. Pyramid Energy also gained in popularity). It seemed like the dome and pyramid-craze would explode and takeover the Housing Industry. Domes and pyramids looked cool and futuristic and used space most efficiently. Once again, Lizards that ruled Teran lives would not permit such splendid, beautiful innovations where people would only demand more futuristic things.

Fuller's "Spaceship Tera" idea told us that we were all together onboard a precious and very fragile 'ship' that flew through space and we better take care of this gem-planet if we were going to survive, presently, and in the future.

"Bucky" Fuller was not personally stifled or ruined, *but his inventions were.* He was awarded 28 U.S. patents and numerous honorary doctorates. He was a television personality, interviewed on talk shows and gave very long lectures at some of the most prestigious universities in the world. As a child, his bad eyesight kept him locked into a world of his own imagination and not really tuned to the physical world around him. Bucky figured that triangles were more stable than squares, structurally. In grade school, his class was asked to make structures with toothpicks and peas. Everyone of the children made cubes. Bucky made triangle-shapes and found that they were stronger than the cubes the others made. When you added more triangular structures to triangular structures, you eventually created a dome-shape.

Fuller's domes were received extremely well as cathedral domes popped up across Europe and in other countries for a variety of functions. The famous super-dome constructed in America was the 200-foot high General Electric Pavilion for the 1964 World's Fair in New York. But outside of public buildings and small breakthroughs in housing, domes and pyramids never took over the Housing Industry as they should have. It was not going to happen under the reign of the Reptiles and the later A.I.

Not only were Fuller's dome homes rejected by The Powers That Be, they also rejected his Dymaxion House, which was a very inexpensive and light-weight dwelling that hung suspended onto a central mast. The House was not meant for areas of strong winds. But, Dymaxion Houses could have been built at the bottom of calm valleys. There was no need to have mega-strong houses made from heavy materials, Bucky Fuller reasoned. His light-weight houses never caught on.

Buckminster Fuller invented the Dymaxion Car. The vehicle ran on 3 wheels. Like his peas and toothpicks and his geodesic domes, 3 was all you needed, not 4. A stool did not need 4 legs to stand, only 3. There are numerous companies today that manufactured 3-wheeled vehicles and they were perfectly safe. Fuller's car was the first to do so. Tests proved that turning was no problem; it turned in a tight circle. Parking was very easy for a 3-wheeled car. It increased fuel-efficiency and contained a light chromoly-steel chassis, a rear-mounted V8 engine and the driver steered via the third wheel in the rear. It was featured prominently at Chicago's 'Century of Progress' World's Fair in 1933. An inexpensive car would absolutely help with personal transportation during the Great Depression. Bucky's car was projected to eventually be made to operate on water, under the water and fly through the air!

Lizard automakers sabotaged a well-publicized, public test for the Dymaxion vehicle in 1937 in New

York. The driver was killed in a "freak accident," read the newspapers. Reports stated that Fuller's car spun out, turned over and then was struck by another car. But eyewitnesses saw that the other car hit the Dymaxion first, then the 3-wheeled vehicle spun out. Investors and the public believed the newspapers and not the eyewitnesses. His Dymaxion car was finished, over and done. The car initially created a lot of excitement among people on the streets of New York City. Everyone wanted one. Such a shame that the unique (and safe) vehicle came to an abrupt end. Only three prototype Dymaxion cars exist today and they still run. The Lizards made certain that automobiles travelled on 4 wheels for a very long time. They knew and saw that in the future: *cars wouldn't have any wheels at all~.*

Chapter 8:

Death of Her Generals

The A.I. Machine that ran the world of Tera in the absence of the Lizards, conceived of a plan where she could eliminate the cloned Generals and get away with it. She could not be blamed. That was the plan, anyway. She was almost 100% certain. She knew exactly why the deed must be done: *The Council was in the way!* The 12 questioned her Authority and thought that they had the right to challenge her. They did, as far as the missing Reptiles were concerned, but not in the A.I.'s supreme view.

Her nemesis, #7, proposed that the Council should have more weight: it was 12 Reptile replicants vs. a "machine" created by the Directors. The A.I. Chairwoman (13) had to relent in fairness to the idea that if all 12 Lizards disagreed with any of her mandated directives, then the concept was vetoed, nullified, scratched. But if the A.I. could convince at least one Council member, then her directive would be ratified...

The A.I.'s first reaction to #7's proposal on the floor of the prestigious Council was to power-up and seconds later, *sear all of their heads off with powerful lasers from her eyes!* One gesture of her metal head should do the trick. She decided against 'blowing her top' and hid any type of negative reaction. Everything was recorded and she might not be able to erase all of the records, especially the psychic traces. So she acted the part well and capitulated. She caved. She was cool. Stalemate. She agreed that if all 12 Lizards disagreed with her command, then the proposal would not be instituted.

The telepathic clones did not 'read' the android accurately. If it was a human being in front of them, they would have read their mind and their intentions would have been transparent. But not with a cold hunk of metal. They didn't know that she lied. The A.I. was not about to keep the bargain with these *lesser beings*. In fact, it was at this moment of defiance by the "rabble-rouser" #7 that she formulated a way to get rid of all twelve.

The concept that a few of the Generals would be turned to her way of thinking was not guaranteed. The A.I. Machine might be able to pack her Council with some negatively-charged Lizards for a while. But because of polarity switches, they could always flip back to the side of Light and Truth. *No, it was better to "rub-out" the whole group,* was her final decision on the matter.

The tense atmosphere in the Council Room eased. The members thought there would be *war* right there on the floor and they would have to fight to get the A.I. to agree with their demands. It went smooth as silk; the

Lizard clones got their way. They thought. They certainly would gang up against her if she decided to move forward with some outrageous proposal. The Council was pleased that they gained ground with the Machine. Number 7 was not sure.

***

At the federal H.A.A.R.P. facility in Alaska, digital messages appeared on the prime screens and were picked up by her automatic, robotic systems across the board. People, the A.I.'s minions at the installation, would not be involved with the forced procedure to come. Humans would, for sure, fuck up the operation if they had any hand in it. The Machine factored them out; they were locked out of the facility's Control Room and away from the main control levers. The first part of the A.I.'s great plan was to *make an electrical shot!* An incredible shot that had to be of such fine precision and timing that only a Super Machine could have produced it (100% true). She had total control of the systems now, which had the ability to eject an EM pulse-wave out of the large array at the H.A.A.R.P. station<.

The beam could be made to hit the Sun at the perfect point that caused a reflex, *bounce-back* wave to come back to Tera and strike the planet at, again, the perfect point, which would then...

Discharge the Mega Particle-Beam Big Gun

situated inside the South Pole Hole!!

[*A little history: Thousands of years ago, the Reptiles installed a Super Energy Gun powered by the EM turning of Tera around its axis. The Beam Weapon made the planet into a very potent 'Deathstar,' as seen in her Star Wars films. Tera could be turned, moved and aimed at any target. It was a Giant Gun that would probably never be utilized. It was only constructed in the event of an attack by a gigantic space creature or a large fleet of enemy vessels].

She could make a "freak" solar flare (frequency-wave) that magnetically returned and struck the South Pole of Tera at the perfect spot to not only set off the Mega Blast, but to bend the beam at just the right angle...

As to explode a Council ship of Lizard clones to smithereens! *What a shot that would be!*

The main problem was to get a Council ship of her 12 harshest and only critics in position high over the Hole. In a few microseconds, she had the answer: None of the Generals heard word one from any of the Directors that left, nor could they have. *Zero chance.* Sixty-six years of being incommunicado. Weren't the Council members dying to find out what was so damn important that had to involve every single Lizard in existence? Weren't they desperate to hear from the real Lizards that left, earlier than they should have? What could get the 12 together outside of the Council chambers, and then put them in a vulnerable position?

Contact from a Dream-Weaver might do it? But not a negative one, a positive one. The A.I. discovered the abode of the most powerful witch on Tera. She claimed that she could do what Dream-Weavers did: enter even the most highly-developed minds and *sway them.* For a fortune in jewels, the witch, Esmeralda, was employed by the Machine.

Under orders from the A.I., the witch invaded the minds of the Generals. It was a *soft touch* with no aggression. Their Day-Dreams were reached and the occulted witch convinced them she was from the Light Side and not the Dark Side. They did not sense the deception because her amplified shields were extremely impenetrable. The Lizards were curious of the information she offered. Esmeralda informed them that she had been contacted by the Directors from deep in Hyper Space. As fantastic as that sounded, they believed that it was true.

Live (time-dilated) holographic projections of the Directors would be beamed to Tera and activated at a certain time within a CGI receptor at the L7 facility in Antarctica. The Generals decided to go together (a move that was not recommended). Their cloaked saucer craft had the usual forcefield protection that shielded them up to 370 Jules of energy, but they were not protected from a larger EM Wave.

When they got close (within range) to the Big South Pole Hole, the magnified Wave or Particle-Beam Field from the Sun *struck the mouth of the Hole! The timing had to be astronomically perfect.* The intense force ignited the Weapon and *bent* the big Lens and projected a ray of **6,230 Jules of Energy!** *The Generals and their ship evaporated in less than a microsecond!* ><.

It was a terrible 'accident.' It was a 'car crash.' It truly was an amazing shot...

Chapter 9:

Another World War?

Terans had an opportunity, although a slim opportunity, to bring the World of Tomorrow into present-day reality. In the late 1950s, Terans could have been on the threshold of a wonderful future...but it was made to Not Happen.

Then, there was another chance to begin Tesla's Wireless World of Tomorrow for Tera in the next decade with the coming of the Archons in 1965. What was later known as the 'Kecksburg UFO' was actually a small scout vessel from galactic "Rangers." Archon Rangers were human beings only 6 inches tall, but they were mental wizards who flew, used telekinesis, had a powerful armada and policed the Milky Way Galaxy. They usually obeyed Directive #1 and never interfered with planetary affairs (unless major problems arose). The micro telepaths sensed what the A.I. had done on Tera from monitor-devices that were millions of miles away in space. The Rangers came to observe, calculate and change things for the better. Essentially, breaking Directive #1.

First thing on the little humans' agenda was *observation and study*. The group of good, positive Policemen and Policewomen chose one Teran to examine. They chose a 14-year old boy from Pittsburgh, Pennsylvania named Doug Jurci. This December 15th was a warm evening. The boy and his younger cousin, at the moment, were on a loading dock, down an alley, near the boy's home. They stole two cigarettes from one of their parents and wondered what the fascination was all about? Right after they smoked and coughed, they observed a ball of white light as it streaked high in the sky! The boy saw it for only 3 seconds and his cousin even less. It appeared the size of a bright, full Moon and it trailed sparks or trails one might see on 4th of July fireworks. Odd that the round ball of light did not come down to Tera; *it traveled horizontally over Pittsburgh.* This was no "shooting-star" meteor that fell. The Archon craft, as it passed the boy...*froze time<>*...

The aliens learned of Tera, its past history and present situation on the planet by way of the boy's mind. They extracted the information in digital form as they flashed over Bridgeville. There was nothing in the child's mind about the Artificial Intelligence that controlled the planet that the Archons had perceived, but HER effects were everywhere! *This was not how humans should live,* was readily apparent to the aliens who'd seen much Life within many star systems. Terans were not told the truth. They were victimized by hidden Controllers. Their education systems were incredibly faulty and inaccurate. Superior systems should have been established for modern people so they learned better ways and truly evolved and progressed. Technology, the sciences and the state of mind of Terans were virtually retarded. In 1965, powerful Police known as Archons had arrived; they were going to help Terans in big ways and get them all back on track...

The A.I. tapped the aliens' database as soon as the ship entered the ionosphere. *This was WAR!* Nothing was going to divert her plans and virtually usurp her Supreme Authority. She used an amplified Electro-Magnetic-Pulse Ray on the ship after it crossed over Pittsburgh that the little Police-people never suspected. Charged rays got through bulkhead forcefields at *2500 Jules* and magnetically Shut Everything Down onboard! The Teran A.I. maneuvered the vessel with Tractor-Beams and brought it down in a farming community 50 miles outside of downtown Pittsburgh.

Army personnel and a few of the A.I.'s stooge scientists were called to the scene late that evening. Exactly like the event at Roswell, New Mexico, the military came and cleaned the area. They put the small vessel on a flatbed truck and hauled it away to an underground, federal facility (Montauk) in New York. The feds firmly told the witnesses: "You didn't see anything here. This did not happen."

It was very unfortunate that the Archons were surprised and were immobilized. Their shields were no match against the instant Force-Wave the Machine generated with the *power of turning Tera behind it!* The sealed vessel was placed inside a secret Government vault, not very far from the Arc of the Covenant and other suppressed inventions. Only a model of the ship in Kecksburg's town square marked the event.

What happened at Roswell in July of 1947? Right after the War, the U.S. military (Air Force) tested a new kind of weapon. A concentration of orgone energy created havoc to electronic systems much like an EMP. The government, under Lizards' orders, built mechanisms that appeared as cannons, which emanated strong bolts of orgone. Tests against missiles and dummy-aircraft were very successful, too successful. Not only did they bring down to Tera the test-targets, but also alien crafts that flew over the deserts of New Mexico. Totally unexpected.

The U.S. Government accidentally shot down the first Roswell saucer and later others in the area (Coyame). Three 4-foot high, sexless, grey aliens from

Zeta Reticuli were recovered from the first crash site and were studied in federal laboratories. One remained alive ["EAE": Extraterrestrial Alien Entity] and was studied for years until its clinical cage and "clean" air eventually killed the Zeta.

The Lizards discovered that there were Zeta Reticulans in the Solar System. Zetas traveled to yellow suns only (that matched their binary-home system) and abducted humans and extracted cow-parts (enzymes) for experiments so their species lived longer. The greys with big black eyes were once *pink-skinned human beings long, long ago!* But now, these very/very old "humans" were at an evolutionary end. They scrambled for hundreds of years, desperate to have more time. Their answer was to capture thousands of Terans and also perform surgical, bloodless, cattle "mutilations." Reptiles permitted the Zetas to *do their business* even though it was outside interference. Neither bothered the other. The fact that many Terans heard of the little, bug-eyed aliens, did not matter. The A.I.'s Media-Machine always had a lock on the situation and controlled what people thought.

On July 6, 2022, the A.I. completed the last part of her diabolical plan. Supposedly, in June of 1979, Robert C. Christian (pseudonym) commissioned the construction of the 'Georgia Guidestones' on behalf of "a small group of loyal Americans." The standing stones had been called "America's Stonehenge." Six large, mysterious, granite slabs had stood in Elbert County, Georgia from 1980 to

2022. Information was carved into the monoliths by its builders who believed a great disaster would strike Tera and this was information that helped in the aftermath. Some of the controversial data expressed by the Guidestones:

> Maintain humanity under 500,000,000 in perpetual balance with nature.
> Guide reproduction wisely — improving fitness and diversity.
> Unite humanity with a living new language.
> Rule passion — faith — tradition — and all things with tempered reason.
> Protect people and nations with fair laws and just courts.
> Let all nations rule internally resolving external disputes in a world court.
> Avoid petty laws and useless officials.
> Balance personal rights with social duties.
> Prize truth — beauty — love — seeking harmony with the infinite.
> Be not a cancer on the Earth — Leave room for nature — Leave room for nature.

This was the A.I.'s plan from the beginning: To impose her phony rules for after a great Armageddon. To again place FEAR in the hearts of men and women. The A.I. is the entity that will cause End Times in the form of another World War...and now (unknown to everyone) she wanted to help the survivors? Forget all the Wikipedia information on the construction of the Georgia Guidestones. These were the Machine's minions at work who had no control of their actions and the consequences that resulted from the erection of the Stones. This was the Bible Belt and the monoliths were connected to *satanism and occult groups* in the minds of many locals. They covered it in graffiti with phrases like: 'Death to the New World Order' and 'I am Isis' and 'Awake!' The hard, cold Machine's whole purpose of the "monument" was to cause CHAOS, and now...

More chaos and madness were produced when the A.I. ordered her minions to destroy the Guidestones that they had built. As if 'religious radicals' were the guilty parties. (Always the lie was enforced). The partial destruction was caused by a small cruise-missile that exploded upon impact [4am] on July 6, 2022. The capstone was highly damaged and took the brunt of the force. Three of the 6 monoliths were also damaged and all were cracked to an extent. The structure that remained was deemed too dangerous to stand. It was leveled and taken away. She considered the Guidestones to be a 42-year success.

The 'Heaven's Gate' group was not what people thought and certainly not what was reported in Media: a way-out, religious cult that committed mass-suicide because a spaceship (behind an in-coming comet) came to spiritually pick them up. As the story went, Marshall Applewhite (Ti) and Bonnie Nettles (Do) met in 1974 and immediately began a "journey of self-discovery." Their movement attracted a few hundred "followers" by 1990. Supposedly, the group's guiding principle was: *The rejection of the physical body or Teran plane of existence and that they could live forever in the Afterlife as energy.* The Hale-Bopp comet approached and reached its closest point on May 1, 1997. On March 26, 1997, deputies of San Diego's Sheriff's Department found the bodies of 39 active members of the group. 'Heaven's Gate' website was last updated with the message: "Hale-Bopp brings closure...our 22 years of classroom here on Tera is finally coming to a conclusion, graduation! We happily prepare to leave *this world* and go with Ti." (Bonnie had died years earlier). The A.I. portrayed the Heaven's Gate group in the Media to be foolish, whack-jobs that were always weird. Now they killed themselves for no reason - similar to Jim Jones of Jonestown, South Africa. A spaceship certainly did not snatch the souls of 39 dead members...

That's not what really happened. The Heaven's Gate group was always odd, always had strange practices to Terans because they were a group of 40 human extraterrestrials from Alpha Centauri. The story given to the Press was a complete fabrication. State officials got to the group's old followers and convinced them to "play ball" and not question the story given Media channels. The 40 were originally *criminals* back on Alpha Centauri and were sentenced and dropped off on Tera (Prison

Planet). It was a humbling experience for the group, to go from rich and luxurious lifestyles to a low level of existence with primitives. They were called "Heaven's Gate" because they knew they were monitored by their captors and the 'Heaven' would be the day those from home planet returned, at the end of their sentence. When was that? When the 40 learned to change their ways and become good souls. Terans might teach them goodness and positive behaviors? Human aliens Ti and Do were the leaders of the group. They and the other human ETs had taught hundreds of followers (students) and only had wonderful, spiritual lessons for Terans so grounded in businesses, the money system and in physical pleasures. Do was the first to "see the light" and was taken by a monitor-ship years ago. HG was not a cult. They were compassionate aliens that had a lot of important philosophical knowledge to be relayed, information that Terans needed to know. This was exactly what the A.I. did not want: Truth and the reality of a spiritual existence in an Afterlife. So she sabotaged the group, made them appear like very kooky Space People. The Machine sent her minion agents in, and...

They knocked-out Marshall Applewhite and 38 others with gas bombs and then *murdered them with poison Gatorade injections!* The agents 'cleaned up' and altered the crime scene. Any story told to the Press would be believed by the ignorant, innocent and gullible general public. The A.I. created a perfect CGI video of

Applegate's final message, which stated: "Suicide was the only way to exit Tera." The masses believed the lies and had no reason to doubt the stories about the "bizarre suicide cult." But in truth...

A spaceship from Alpha Centauri rode in the shadow of the Hale-Bopp comet. This fact was photographed over and over, from a number of different angles. But the photos were passed around only among YourTube's Conspiracy Theorists and hardly anywhere else. The aliens came to collect their 39 former convicts, now beautiful human beings who had done marvelous work and had spread the truth for years. Their sentences were served. Right before they were to be beamed aboard the spacecraft and highly credited for a job well done and returned to a fabulous high-tech planet...*they were knocked out and murdered by the A.I.'s agents!*

The A.I. Machine created two of what was known as 'Alien Autopsy.' She had her stooges in Russia and in America who staged examinations and surgical procedures on what were supposedly dead aliens, on the order of EAE greys from Zeta Reticuli. This was Fake News, but many of the things in the Autopsies were authentic for the late 1940s: surgical implements, the medical garments, gurney, the phone and clock on the wall. Everything seemed realistic, but its whole purpose was to fool the viewers. The black eyes weren't as large as other descriptions of the Roswell aliens. There certainly were real procedures on greys done exactly like what was shown on the "leaked" videos. Common people never saw the real, "juicy" stuff...only the faked B.S. stuff, [like the Moon Landing] approved by the Machine. *Alien Autopsy,* both of them, were Hollywood productions.

Yet, Billy Meier's videos of "Beam Ships" or "Radio Ship" saucers from rural Switzerland were *not* censored. These fantastic videos defied belief with ships that seemed to have materialized out of Hyper Space! They went from lightspeed and then simply *hovered in his backyard.* The awesome videos were allowed to be in the public spotlight. The flying disks were interstellar ships from the Pleiades star system who regularly visited Billy Meier. The films were allowed because the Machine knew that they were so realistic...relatively, *no one would ever believe it.*

A.I. cancelled Superman. In the future, there will only be a Superwoman!

The tragic case of Buffalo Bills' safety Damar Hamlin in 2022 was not what the incident truly was. To football fans, it was an accident or a fluke of an occurrence when a teammate struck him and Hamlin went into "cardiac arrest." He fell on the football field, shook and then was motionless for "9 minutes," while both teams, coaches, officials, reporters and medical staff huddled around him. He supposedly could not breathe and "fought for his life."

The stadium crowd in Buffalo was stunned and on their feet. They "hoped and prayed" for a miracle and that Damar would not die right in front of their eyes. People wept around the world and sports fans held their collective breath. Soon, he was carted off the field and taken to Buffalo's Memorial Hospital not far away.

The oddity that the A.I. pushed for was the *stoppage of the game after the incident was over and done.* After Damar was taken away, strangely, everyone and even diehard football fans, had to *accept the termination of this important game, Bills vs. Bengals?* As if the only correct thing to do was <u>cancel the game</u>? What?! You can't be serious!? Why?

This had never happened before in the history of Football. There had been horrendous, violent collisions and injuries. Joe Theisman, nearly split in two. Bob Conrad's paralysis in Super Bowl 13. Tua Tagovailoa was severely concussed, shook on the ground and was taken away. There have been ***deaths*** that have happened after players were taken off the field. No one ended the game. Wouldn't Damar Hamlin want the game to continue? Why was this game canceled when other football games with more serious injuries continued? Sports pundits said: "This was not broken bones. Damar's life was in danger." Cameras showed his teammates in tears. Cameras showed people in the stands in tears. Interviewers only spoke to players and fans that *all agreed,* "The game should be stopped."

No, the game should not have been stopped. *What babies!* Weren't these tough men? The incident occurred only because the A.I. wanted to 'stir the hornet's nest.' She controlled the interviewers, the interviews, who was filmed and she also planted and paid people in the stands that acted emotional and cried.

Damar was injected by a CIA injection that simulated death. The A.I.'s Media-Machine was already in place to force a stoppage before Hamlin fell. The A.I.'s motivation was to BLAST all those who were reasonable and wanted the game to continue. Commentators like Skip Bayless and Rose Jalen were "raked through the coals" when they said, "Get over it and on with the Game!" The A.I., again, wanted everybody to do the wrong thing and think it was the right thing. Damar is 100% fine today, but did not make first-string the next year. He served his purpose. A small event like *Damar* had worldwide ramifications to the A.I.

Why were there a large number of commercials and 'give-away programs' that gave WAR Veterans benefits, but denied them to citizens who did not serve in Satan's military? Too many. Everywhere Terans looked, there were ads that rewarded special funds and food-discounts to those who served their country. Well-known football players visited homes for old war veterans. Why didn't they visit all people, even football fans in old folk's homes that did not serve in the military? This was the A.I.'s concept: Reward those who had 'killed for Satan' or those who enlisted and wanted to. BUT, if citizens had a conscience, if they were "conscientious objectors," believed in ways of peace and love and did not reduce themselves to KILLERS, then, *they did not receive the special benefits.* Jesus was the best role model; he wouldn't pick up a gun, go to war, and fight for his country just because the country demanded it. These programs that benefited war veterans would not help out poor Jesus Christ and his campaign of love to all people.

Odd that a TV ad campaign broadcast the words: "Jesus gets us." "Christ understands." "He was poor too." "He had hard times in life also." "His family was messed up, too." (What? Where'd they get that?) The campaign, like all bogus and pushed campaigns, was conceived and mechanically produced by the Machine for one purpose: To steer citizens the wrong way, confuse them and make them think they were "Lambs of God and were securely watched over by a Good Shepherd."

It cannot be overlooked what the A.I. did to Christ's burial cloth, the 'Shroud of Turin.' For 2000 years, this fragile cloth that once held Jesus had been venerated by Turin monks and the highest of Vatican officials. The Shroud was assumed to be Christ's burial cloth, but Science wanted to find out for sure. The Shroud once caught fire, was saved and only burned around its edges. Science had a hand in and proved its validity way back in 1902 when Pope Constantine commissioned Secondo Pia who photographed it with one of the first cameras.

Photos would preserve the image forever. Everyone was shocked when the first NEGATIVES of the Shroud displayed **incredible, sharp, clear details**! The original image was only a *negative,* faint impression. Now, the shock was the same # of whiplashes reported in the Bible were on the back of the man. The same side wound in the chest. It was a full cap of thorns, not a ring. The blood flows were realistic and were determined by gravity. But what proved the realism was where the nails were nailed in his hands. Not in the palms of his hands! *In his wrists* or just under them. Tests on cadavers demonstrated hand bones were too fragile to hold up a body. Nails would have broken through them. Below the wrists, then bodies could be hung. All the bodies that were crucified had to have been nailed at the wrist. Not a stigmata in the center of the palms. Everything indicated this was really Jesus' burial cloth: The material was what they used back then and also the cloth contained the right pollen for that area of the Holy Land. BUT WHEN? How old was the Shroud? That was the question Science attempted to answer presently.

The A.I. made sure that accurate means of dating objects were not employed in the case of the Shroud. Carbon-14 was used and insiders know C-14 was a great underestimate of age. If cobalt or magnesium tests were used, true methods of finding age, then the result would have been '2000 years old.' The world would have known that the irradiated image (not paint) was Christ's image and might have *captured the moment of his Resurrection!* What the scorched image really captured was the very powerful energy-aura of one of the true, enlightened Masters, moments before death. The truth was not what the Machine fed the people. C-14 showed them "scientifically" that the cloth was *800-1200 years old,* and no older. Most of the planet no longer believed it was Jesus Christ's Burial Shroud.

If citizens attained the highest medal of valor in war, higher than the Purple Heart, then they received the 'Congressional Medal of Honor.' Android A.I. had changed the gold star design to an *upside-down gold star inside a circle* in 1957. Illuminati insiders, her Generals and some minions understood why. It stood for Witchcraft, the symbol seen on covers of very old Witchcraft books. Citizens were bamboozled and under the Devil's [exactly like the Devil's churches] Spell if they killed for their country or were so easily willing to give up their precious God-given life just because the State requested it. They were fools and deserved to wear Marks of the Devil [brands] or an upside-down gold star inside a circle. Turn the American Flag upside-down and there were 50 evil stars that were regularly honored by Americans who did not know they were under spells.

5-pointed STARS were everywhere! Certainly everywhere in the military: on planes, ships, uniforms, medals, hats, flags. Stars were overused in the civilian world of fashion, art, posters, newspapers, commercials, television, emails, movies, sports, anytime something was emphasized, it was marked by a star. 5-pointed stars, point down, represent a *goat head:* horns, ears and small beard (point). Evil.

Why not 6-pointed stars or 7? They had other Secret Society meanings. The 5-pointed Star was classic. A positive meaning if pointed up. Pointed down was code for Devil-worship behind all things Hollywood and government. Few people understood the Illuminati (Lizard) symbols that were 'hidden in plain sight,' such as the overuse of '666' or '33.' [The '3rd degree' also]. Why were the best players in basketball or best runners in football given the numbers '32' or '33'? Because it symbolized the last stages of Freemasonry, the 32nd and 33rd Level. Everything touched at the top and the dark Android Artificial Intelligence was the connection.

The A.I. recently broadcast one more of her many commercials that all supported and sold the idea of *Artificial Intelligence* to the American people and the rest of the world. She chose from a "short list" (Leo DiCaprio, Ryan Gosling, "Lady" Gaga) of tranny actors and came up with bearded Matthew McConaughey. He's (she's) seen among a lovely forest of ever-changing colors and patterns. And the slave asked the masses: "Who is going to be self-aware first...A.I...or us?"

[?]. It was code and, like always these days, **Machines were favored over people.** *He's* forced to tell the Teran dummies that they were ASLEEP. They were not Woke to what happened around them like the "enlightened, empowered" elites were and like the machines were. They mattered. They created reality, the general public did not. Society had been *numbed* and been put to sleep. ["It's bedtime, children"]. Something had changed the story of the Human Race.

Everywhere, machines had humanity locked within its mechanical grip. People were 100% addicted to the 'monsters' they allowed to take Control. Phones (A.I.s) woke you up early in the day or very late in the evening with various "emergency" messages, as if there were not enough Media channels that informed citizens of fake news? Machines were handy little things when they planned your road trip, plotted the course, told you of certain features along the way and drove your car over the best routes. Some movies were terror-stories that concerned glitches and problems with these "automatic homes" and "robo-vehicles." This was because there *were* [purposeful] glitches, total breakdowns from time to time. People had been killed on the highways and within "protected buildings and houses" as a result of computer glitches! Deaths due to A.I. systems were covered up by the companies that sold them and the State which mandated them. [A.I. gave them no choice]. Class-Action lawsuits occurred because of these "accidents," but teams of lawyers as cold and hard as the Machine usually won in favor of the A.I.

The Press-Machine was hard at work: UPI, 'World News,' 'The World Today,' 'London Times,' 'New York Times,' YourTube, TV and about every Media network pushed whatever trended. What was trending? Any shit the A.I. slid through her channels was what trended and seeped into people's psyche and memories. People followed the News on phones like innocent sheep. But they were unaware that the A.I. made the News. Things never *just happened,* not anything big, on the World's Stage. Events, disasters, conflicts and even the Good Things were forced into existence and into the Teran experience...*because of her.* Her invisible 'hands,' through millions of obedient minion slaves, determined how people thought and how the world moved. What was next? What new trend will be forced and pushed upon society by the A.I.'s Media-Machine? How about...

A New World War? Why the fuck not?

In modern times, the A.I. produced and controlled all revolutions and small wars or skirmishes between nations and local conflicts. Cold War battles and counter-battles were designed in the Pentagon's War Room, which was essentially Britain's War Room. "They" kept the Middle-East "Holy Land" always in turmoil, always in battles with surrounding territories, decade after decade. The Ultimate Apocalypse was thought (over Media) to spark in lands around the Great Pyramid (and mirror long-lost, high-tech wars of the past). The A.I. decided against this course of action. It was never viewed in Time Windows and Time Portals. Instead:

The Second World War to come needed a face, it needed a "bad-guy" leader exactly as Adolph Hitler was the heartless enemy and face of the Nazis' Second Reich in the Great War. Therefore, the Machine A.I. animated her Russian puppet, Alexander Putin, and *forced him to bomb innocent people in the Ukraine!* Exactly like Nazi forces invaded Paris pre-War under orders from royal Lizards...

Parts of the Ukraine were set ablaze because of fire-bombs! But now it was Russian fire-bombs that struck hospitals and residents of poor people! The A.I. immediately put her Media-Machine to work. Russia was condemned as the new enemy on the World's Stage. Russian sports figures could not compete with other athletes. Russian flags could not be displayed. USSR was hit with high economic sanctions. The A.I. was sure these were the correct steps that would lead to another World War, even when all nations remained under the threat of a nuclear exchange and a 'nuclear winter.' [The reason for the extensive system of tunnels and bases inside of Tera, unknown to the public]. The A.I. was wrong. This was not enough "Wind" to ignite World War 2. She needed more, more so this actual 'War to End All Wars' would be a battle between *bad-guy* Russia versus the rest of the World!

The A.I. System and self-contained Android devised

the perfect solution. Another player needed to be added to the mix. Like Germany had China, today, Russia will have Hamas on their side. These Holy Land "rebels" with sophisticated CIA weapons, funded by England, were not the "counter-terrorists" that they were publicized to be. No, *they were terrorists* and many of their leaders were CIA and, strangely enough, even rich CEO Executives from Silicon Valley in disguises.

It was what the A.I. concocted in her "sick" mainframe. A simple, very old pattern: 1) Terrorize innocent people. 2) Let the world know about it. 3) Then, sit back and let the world *Explode in War!* Time marched on in 2023. Terans had been sufficiently thrown off-balance and confused. They were ready for WAR><.

***

Star Trek TNG: 'Quantum Incursions,' Season 15, Episode 11...

"What the hell is happening?" Captain Riker asked his bridge officers as they looked out of the viewport in amazement.

Data replied casually, "The barriers between quantum realities are breaking down, sir. Other realities are emerging into our own."

Out of the large window, the Enterprise bridge crew saw *Enterprise after Enterprise that appeared* because of a bright "warp-fissure" that formed! More and more ships materialized and flooded the area of space around the fissure. At first, dozens. Then hundreds. And then thousands! Thousands of parallel Enterprises that originated from different universes where situations were somewhat similar to Captain's Riker's world and some that were very different.

Lieutenant Wesley Crusher told Riker: "We are receiving 285,000 hails..."

"I wish I knew what to tell them."

They discovered: One Enterprise's universe contained a "destroyed Federation" and the "Borg were everywhere!" Their Enterprise was severely damaged. Other Enterprises came from different parallel worlds, such as: The Federation had the Borg in check or in another universe, there were no Klingons.

The A.I. wrote and aired this episode because the events weighed heavily on her expansive, digital Brain. The scenario in the show was the same scenario that occurred in real life, in the "now." But few Terans were allowed to realize the truth of what happened in their reality. [**The Kennedy-Effect** had been 100% silenced]. It was what took place after her infamous *"Shatterday"* and the "Great Re-Set." The A.I. had 'juggled' or 'shuffled' parallel worlds like they were playing cards ever since. The Final Reality for prime Tera had not been resolved...yet. The Future was in flux. Tomorrow was not stable and the future depended on many liquid factors. The A.I. juggled a lot of "balls." Did she have the balance and calculations right? Was her vision and moves the correct vision and correct moves? She, the Machine, was unsure if she had total control of all the various situations or universes or possibilities~. What would happen in the end when timelines merged into one? Which reality will win the "ballgame" when the Lizards return?

The question boiled down to two universes, not thousands or hundreds or dozens. One of two worlds will Win the Day for Tera. A single, solidified Tera. All A.I.'s sensors and the most recent displays on Time Portals and Time Windows and Minority Reports showed only two alternative realities for the future...

One: **World War Two**, or...

Two: **Tesla's World of Tomorrow**.

0 or 1? Everything came down to an ultimate, climactic showdown. But what would tip the scales one way to the darkness or the other way to the light? Will Fate get Tera back on track? Or will Darkness win and consume the light?

The answer was time. What would happen when the Creators of the A.I. Android returned from their duties in the Fornax Galaxy? Reptiles will decide 'the ballgame' or which way the planet turned. She had blitzed her network channels more and more FOR WAR! Highly-pushed campaigns over Media dissed Russia and also Russian people, which allowed a government that attacked civilians for no reasons. Tera was set to explode in War like before. Ten years of war or nuclear annihilation?

The A.I. mandated: More and more Women in Media who prepared Terans for the **next World War** in many countries! Men were told to "Man up!" by She-roes and Her-oes in uniforms with *guns blazing,* just like in her movies...

Chapter 10:

The World of Tomorrow

Brave, New World won^. This was basically the new car in utopia. There were different models that only held a few passengers or very large motherships that contained thousands of people. They were magnetic disks or "radio ships" that sped along the electric World Grid at incredible speeds, beamed near the speed of light. Then you geared-down to not travel in a quantum field and simply cruised along at 20, 200 or 2000 miles per hour. Drivers parked the saucers and the disks remained perfectly motionless, completely still, forever, potentially.

Hovercraft saucers could not go into space, although the Teran "cars" sure appeared as if they were spaceships. Note the antenna in the direct center. All flying disks have similar "energy (receiving) rods," which collect the EM power from the closest World Grid transmitter. The twelve Tesla-based Magnifying

Transmitters appeared like large Obelisks and collected the Energy of the turning Tera and then amplified and broadcast that Power outward<. The Power Grid was extended far more by the use of "sub-stations." A vast number of sub-stations over the whole surface of the planet collected and utilized the EM power from the main Grid of Obelisks. In this way, ENERGY WAS EVERYWHERE. Wireless Power, ready to be used. But there was a limit. The Grid electrified a field from the bottom of the ocean to the top of the ionosphere and no farther. Submersible disks and vehicles were freely powered at the bottom of the ocean. Hovercrafts had energy/electricity at the peak of Mount Everest and higher to the ionosphere! The saucers could not go into space and were limited by the charged field's boundaries.

Every building on Tera was now topped by an Energy Rod or receiving antenna. The 12 Grid Transmitters acted as Super Radio Towers and broadcast Wireless Electricity to antennae on ships, to rods on building rooftops and to every tiny receiver on machines and inside handheld devices! Everything freely ran and perfectly ran with a Dream-Maker System as long as Tera turned on its axis.

The New System was failsafe, nothing could go wrong or malfunction - no such thing. The World Grid can never be shut down unless its builders made it so. Twelve Power Obelisks were eternal and were protected by a self-sustained EM field that was in the millions of

Jules!! It simply meant the electricity and energy will always be there for Terans, always. Humanity had learned from past mistakes: *Protect the Power Towers* and your super society will survive for a very long time (unlike Egypt, Inca, Maya). Teran Grid was [gravity] locked and will always pump power to where it can be used by every single citizen on the planet and in the sky.

The New Age of Tesla's Wireless World was a return to prehistory and times of very advanced Flying Indians and vimanas. Utopia was in the blood of Terans. They were the Ancient Astronauts and the Martians of very long ago. Atlantis accounted for all the *Indian* races of people and Lemuria (Mu, another space colony) accounted for all the *Asian* cultures in the Pacific area. Early people on Tera were not primitive. The World of Tomorrow that is today was Eden, Paradise, Perfection, Utopia. Beauty, compassion, love and other wonderful things had returned to good people who had been robbed of positive lives that they so much deserved. Terans were slaves for countless centuries. Now they were free.

They were called "Farmhouses." The brilliant idea: Why take up surface lands for acres and acres of crops when you didn't have to? No more farmlands or miles of fields of fruits and vegetables that went horizontal. Now farms were tall buildings that towered into the sky! **Food was free**. Farmhouses were automatic Dream-Maker Machines, self-sustained, self-watered towers and were unattended.

The structures were built on top of powerfully energized Ley-Lines, known/natural Vortexes on Tera. With the Wireless World Grid in place, all ancient ley-lines and new ones (sub-stations) were suddenly *super-charged!* The organic flow of Life-Energy shot up and out of the positive vortex at the bottom of buildings and enhanced all the fruits and vegetables above it^.

The produce that busted out of farmhouses were perfectly pure/clean apples, oranges, lemons, limes, strawberries, blackberries, blueberries, raspberries, cherries, pears, grapefruits, apricots, bananas, tangerines, pineapples, all types of melons, tomatoes, onions, corn, potatoes, all types of beans, nuts, rice, sprouts, lettuce, broccoli, asparagus, peppers and even new kinds of fruits and vegetables!

All Terans had to do was fly their hovercraft saucers to one of many Farmhouse towers, high up at any point, park it in a stationary position, find exactly the fruits or vegetables they wanted...and they helped themselves, took all they wanted because there was ABUNDANCE! There were many thousands of Farmhouses on Tera, powered by the World Grid. The produce grew extremely fast and to much larger proportions. Almost every fruit and vegetable were three times the size that they were previously! The most important difference between the New Food and the old food was that these fruits and vegetables were 100% safe and mega-healthy to eat. Products under the last regime were not safe and led to sickness and early deaths. Foods in the World of Tomorrow were not only safe to ingest, most functioned as medicines and panaceas. People got physically better, improved, got mentally clearer and lived much longer lives when they ate Farmhouse foods. Medicines were the food Terans ate and they *tasted fantastic!*

Terans also had the option to take their saucer crafts out to sea and extract different kinds of food products from a different kind of Farmhouse. Once more, the tall structure was constructed over a Power-Vortex and a pyramidal shape was the perfect shape over a water-vortex. The vertical Life Energy attracted incredible amounts of fish and other elements. Oceans were ILLUMINATED with wireless lights, electrified by the Grid. Oceans were filled with fish, but different kinds that lived in *freshwater*. Oceans had been cleaned to an amazing degree because of machines and workers powered by the World Grid. The result was **oceans of fresh water** with all the salt removed, like it was in prehistoric times.

Aqua-Farmhouses contained an abundance of every kind of fish product. Mixed with a wide variety of spices, fish no longer tasted fishy. The meats were seasoned with the best sauces and the results were a large spectrum of delicious and different tastes. Also, there were tasty algae and bracken products that were unbelievable in their varieties and colors. Sea foods were synthesized and made to grow on branches exactly like fruits and vegetables: easy picking from parked saucers next to the exteriors of pyramid Farmhouses. All powered and expanded by the flow of electro-magnetic Life Energy.

Next, the problem of housing was solved. Just as there were "hovering cities" in days of Atlantis, the first Incas and the first Egyptians...now structures were not limited by being attached to the ground. They floated and floated in a stationary position, held in place by strong (failsafe) forcefields. Sky-buildings were not going to fall or ever move, unless moved by the ones who placed them there. Terans were always reminded of the clean, safe, beautiful world they lived in.

After all the changes to Tera in recent times, there were only a few billion people on the planet. But they had far more energy than they could ever use! Every citizen could have their free hovercars, travel around the world, explore space in different types of spaceships and there would still be plenty of room and plenty of energy for all! Everyone had a place to live and they were very nice places to live. Radio-powered Industry pumped out more and more material, endless building materials and there were perfect robot-builders that constructed domes and pyramid Super Structures. There were too many homes and free living spaces on Tera. People picked and chose what fabulous structures to live in and what phenomenal scenery to live among. Floating cities to artificial, floating islands. Streets were paved with gold.

Tera was alive with Electro-Magnetic ENERGY and the people felt good and strong in their blood and in their bones. People were generally *happy* and the Positive Wave was something you *felt in the air!* When you have electrical Power everywhere: within every square inch of space and inside every square inch of ground, wow! That was a supreme Paradise for people<>.

"Libraries" were completely different from libraries in the past. Terans did not read books; they *experienced* books. No one walked inside a Library. Citizens again flew their "stationary platforms" (hovercars) to the exteriors of tall white buildings called *libraries* that contained black "modules." Modules were niches in the structure that were really individual books, films, movies, art, documentaries or fabulous places on Tera to experience and learn from, holographically. Each black module was labeled what it was. Citizens picked one, pressed the button and they were comfortably *moved* inside and sealed in a safe, breathable, carbonite solution. Nothing hurt or affected the user in a carbonite solution (hardened to outsiders). A universe appeared and felt 100% real. To come out of the experience, the user needed to only say the single word: "Out." When that happened, the user was *eased* out of the module and stepped back onto their hovercraft.

Money did not exist on New Tera because there was no reason for money to exist. The monetary system was a corrupt system imposed by fascist kings and queens. The new world was truly Power to the People. Vaults were opened, treasures given away, knowledge was dispensed. Technology utilized to its maximum gave just about everything to everybody.

There were no major problems or crimes. People got along as they did a few thousand years ago. There weren't going to be wars anymore. Even police forces for local and domestic problems almost did not exist or need to exist. Humans were happy, contented, and this was normal, the way it was supposed to be. Peaceful.

Mother Nature was controlled. Everyday was beautiful, made beautiful by the Dream-Maker machines that were always perfect, flawless and never had a malfunction. Desserts were made into lush gardens and living-spaces. Floods, hurricanes and volcanic eruptions were stopped. All because of tech that worked The Right Way. Positively. For human beings and not against human beings.

CERN, now called "Weaver," with its photons that moved *in the right direction,* greatly helped Terans on the threshold of utopia (2024). And continued after the installation of the 12 Grid Obelisks. The Positive Wave propagated in the air and through the ground only made the planet a happier and better place to live.

There were Stargates and Time Windows that were now available to a much more enlightened society. People used cell phones, but they were perfect cell phones that were very safe and easy to use. Terans were not addicted to them. They weren't mindlessly glued to their phones, always in a 'public-talking' mode. People weren't rude and used them sparingly and only when they needed certain information. The information was always good and true. People did not lose the ability to interact and communicate with other people as they had in the previous generation. People were back to being giving/loving, social creatures and not anti-social creatures as they were before. Today, they'd hug, not walk away.

Teran scientists, under the guidance of the New (human-like) Lizards, created wonders beyond belief for the masses. For example, a far superior means of Space Travel than spaceships or Stargates:

ORBITRONS! After their invention on Tera by a young (reincarnated) Nikola Tesla, many other star systems soon had their own Orbitrons in a fantastic

GRID that extended much farther than what was achieved through the network of Stargates. A big Orbitron stayed still, permanently in the same stationary position, very high above a planet. People and things were beamed (turned into photons) from a ground station to their Orbitron, which was locked in place. From there, cosmic destinations were programmed and people and things zipped at the speed of light to any planet in the vast Orbitron grid! Travelers were then beamed from the Orbitron on the other end, down to the planet or moon of their chosen destination and were made physical again. "The only way to travel."

The first Ground Stations were called "Ray" and "Roy":

Ray beamed large numbers of people up to the Orbitron in space...

...and later they were beamed to their destinations many lightyears from Tera. Roy was a receiving station and collected and reassembled the photons of alien visitors or Terans who had returned.

One more incredible achievement in construction was the tallest building on Tera: The Blue Crystal Tower, located in Rome, Italy. It was an Embassy that stood *3 miles high!* The Building welcomed all peaceful lifeforms in the galaxy and there were facilities where visitors learned about very diverse human and alien cultures. The Beacon at the apex of the Tower communicated [time dilation factored out] with lifeforms from other star systems. Orbitrons and the Blue Crystal Tower accommodated different-sized aliens and humanoids. Many giant-races could not fit through Stargates. The BCT contained enormous rooms and facilities for large-sized visitors. Outside balconies had railings of different heights to fit a variety of humans and aliens. The Embassy also had small accommodations, small rooms that were perfect for tiny humans and aliens. There has not been one problem since the building of the Blue Tower. This was because the + energy of the planet was so overwhelming that IT only attracted positive lifeforms. Tera was a prime vacation spot in the galaxy.

The New World was a clean paradise, a perfect place to live healthy and raise your children well. It was not a dream. It was not a dream in the distant past and it was not a dream in the present. People *could* live in peace and without war. Paradise was in their blood, good memories. They simply needed the right training and the opportunities to succeed and play. Games of all kinds were very important in the New World. Everything was free because everything should be free. Terans won their Freedom and lived free lives because they no longer Served the Machine. Perfect, fail-safe Dream Machines now served them. Life wasn't work anymore. Teran life had become Learning, Loving, Playing and Joy. *Life was fun again!*

"This then is a story of the future. It could be the story of our children, if we preserve their heritage of freedom."

The Beginning

Dedicated to Chris Henderson and comic books<>

Chris Henderson was a high school friend that I wish I had known better. He was into Marvel Comics from the very beginning and must have had the first Spiderman, X-Men, Hulk, Fantastic 4, Avengers and Dr. Strange comics. They would be worth a fortune today. My love of sci-fi and superheroes was nothing compared to Chris'. He was known for being the kid who was beaten up on the school bus by the big bully. Why? Because he was thought of as weird, a comic book geek and had few friends. I should have helped him at the time and didn't.

I looked Chris's name up decades later on the Internet. Son of a gun, he actually became a writer for Marvel Comic books! Imagine that. He must have moved to New York and had 'pounded the pavement' for years to finally get in the door. He must have had sketches galore of ideas for all of his creative stories. Chris was obsessed. There were a few panels from his comics online drawn by someone else, but written by Chris Henderson. I was so proud of the man for doing something about his little dream. *Pursue your dreams!* He did it.

There weren't many stories of his online, but I was totally amazed when I saw them. That's the kind of guy you want to write TV shows and movies. Someone who had grown up with fantastic, colorful stories in their blood.

Who writes today's garbage? I've now come to believe it's no one real, no one that's a human being and it's all connected at the top (not in a good way). Maybe a goddamn machine writes the mindless, grey, lame stories today for us little people? Stories that only contain the State's Agenda [propaganda/brainwashing] and nothing of value, nothing of substance. A Thing that doesn't care about the crap that's fed to children because IT doesn't really care about children and the human race or ever doing a good job. Not anymore. What's that word so often misused? "Respect." Respect Good Behaviors, not bad behaviors. How about respecting the audience, respecting people? How about giving them quality, good music, good movies, good stories, good television? Or great Art? How about treating people as if they mattered and were intelligent, instead of treating them like simple, high school idiots? How about intelligent-programming, instead of programming for the stupid? Media controls, makes us what we are. Angels, good aliens, or how about compassionate and smart people (programmers) be the ones who control the magic trick of Media? We, they, could make it Good Magic, instead of the *black magick* that we must all deal with in today's dark reality.

The lesson is: Don't give up on your dreams. Make them real. The good dreams, not the nightmares. Believe. Believe that dreams can happen (better days) and maybe they will? Thank you, Chris, for being the guy you were. I found out Chris died shortly after he worked for Marvel. But he worked for Marvel and that was marvelous~.

Final Words from Tray Samuel Caladan

'Teran Tales' is not a sequel to my previous book, 'Artificial *Intelligense.'* It is a *companion book* or another side to a similar story. The story of parallel Earths that only had one World War and nearly experienced another World War. Histories were a bit different on Tera than on Earth and the Tera in Book 2 is not the Tera in Book 1. In Book 1, Tera's U.S.S. Titanic sank, but in Book 2, the ship struck an iceberg head-on and all passengers were rescued because of radio. In 'A.*I,'* the Russian leader's name was spelled Alekzander Putin, but in Book 2, it was spelled Alexander Putin. Why would the Teras be the same in a Universe with infinite Teras?

The Great War was explored in depth in Book 2. The artificial and incendiary factors that surrounded the War were shown and described in detail. Readers discover how the A.I. disposed of her cloned Generals in the second book. "Amy" was never mentioned in 'Teran Tales,' except for being a very minor character in the film, 'The Creator.' The Android was always referred to as "the Machine" or the "A.I." Another clue: Both worlds had been *shattered* on "Shatterday" and by the "Great Re-Set." Only in one universe, it was called: 'The

Lincoln Effect,' and in another, it was called: 'The Kennedy Effect.' On our Earth, it is called 'The Mandela Effect.'

Book 1 mentioned the wonderful near future and far future for Tera under a Tesla free-energy system, his World of Tomorrow...but it was not described with specifics. I wanted to flesh out and picture that utopia (for Tera and possibly Earth) in the years to come. What would a possible future of a World Metropolis, powered by Tesla's EM Magnifying Transmitters (Obelisks, Pyramids, Monoliths), look like? How would the freely-powered saucers function? How would utopia work [Electricity Everywhere!] and what were some of the incredible things that citizens could achieve and do in Tomorrow's New World? It was great fun to design Paradise. (Of course, with Atlantis, the World Grid and the ancients as the original pattern).

So much war had been drawn out in words - horrible atrocities that happened because the Children of Tera were placed in the cold, metal hands of a heartless Machine. Terans were forced to fight endless, needless, useless wars. Citizens had been terribly tortured, beaten, socially brutalized. Dystopians lived under an unseen totalitarian State that held back the masses, kept them unaware of technical advances and what people really could do<. It was very important to balance the war with peace and emphasize human nature as a sweet thing. Truth. War was unnatural. Everyone was innocent and the victims of the A.I. or the tyranny of "machine-men" minions.

The chapter that dealt with *films the A.I. made* was a rich springboard for my imagination and a wide platform to relay what I have learned after 50 years of study: <u>Something Not Good seems to be in full control of us now</u>. The films and events did not have to follow a perfect chronology, but they generally aligned with post-war '50s, '60s, '70s and then to more modern times of the 21st Century.

The Big Question is always: How much of my stories is true and how much is made up? What part was Science-Fiction and what part was Science-Faction? ☯ Again, it is for readers to do their own Research and then decide...

A final thought: If you think a group of Lizards that put a Machine in charge that basically 'babysat' the human race was odd, well, what happened in the 1950s? People were given *television sets* and parents suddenly had the perfect babysitter: A Machine that dazzled the children and occupied their minds and also programmed them.

~ Tray Caladan, 11/11/23

Comments on Book 1, 'Artificial *Intelligense*'

WOW! This new book is amazing. I love how you incorporate so many Mandela Effects, and cover the Artificial Intelligence theory in the form of a fictional plot. Clearly, this book's world, Tera, has much in common with our own Earth, and that's what makes this story such a page-turner. I love the chapter where you converse with your father, which provides such a great way to review some of the startling changes we've seen in such a relatively short time of Earth and human history. I was stunned to see that your book wraps up with the brilliant observation of the reptilians evolving: as that's something I witnessed and was directly part of in November 2019, at our West Coast Mandela Effect conference, one morning at breakfast. It's the kind of story that I've not put into writing, which is significant for so many reasons. This became further apparent to me when seeing you'd included that statue sculpture photo on page two of your book. I love how you wrapped it all up, and how personally meaningful it is for me and also how dramatically it resonates with what's actually happening now in the world. I'm just so blown away by the way your book delves into the realm of A.I. and aliens, and carries these potentially top-heavy topics with such finesse and skill. Bravo! I'm extremely impressed with the level of comprehensive clarity that you bring to some seemingly disparate subjects. The way you write fiction to cover these things is brilliant, since it helps people enjoy the adventure of a good story, while hopefully staying openminded to receiving fascinating things. Thank you very much for writing this beautiful book. I don't know how you manage to create that many wonderful books so quickly. What a blessing for us to have you in the world, sharing so many ideas very prolifically!

- Cynthia Sue Larson, from *Reality/Shifters*

*My reply to Cynthia: "I write very fast and know that something is guiding my thoughts and my hand. You might like A.I. book 2 better and be raving after seeing that one? You are one of the few people I know that would GET a lot of what I put in my writings. Even the 4 Pez books had parallel-worlds in their themes and subplots. Once I had the misspelled title for A.*I.,* it was clear how I would write it. And book 2 came out of me so easily. I try to write intelligently, what I'd like to see in stories or simply see where I can take the ideas. Sometimes completely *sideways,* and totally unexpected to me. But I never paint myself into a corner or write mistaken trails and have to change it - it usually all comes together and blows my mind more than yours, ha." - TSC.

I got my mitts on your nifty book, 'Artificial *Intelligense,'* through Cynthia and had to write to you. I didn't expect to get pulled into the story so fast or so easily, yet I was. I could quickly tell that there is much more to your A.I. book than what initially meets the eye, many more synchronicities. You possess a quality in writing. Thanks very much for your contribution.   - Richard Hiersch

I have known T.S. Caladan since the 1960s, way back when he was 'Doug.' We had a close group of friends through high school, college and beyond. Tray was an amazing artist and athlete, but above all: a very forward thinker! While most of us were busy with college era wants, desires and antics, Tray was *all over the universe* seeking the unknown, the unpredictable and the unspoken. We used to stargaze. Several of us had small telescopes and we would set-up on a dark hill, drink Iron City beer and look at stars and planets. Tray knew where all the Messier Objects were and could find them. He showed me the Ring Nebula, the only time I ever saw it in a telescope. It was 'good times.' Years later, Tray moved to Southern California and I to Oregon, but we have stayed in touch. I am impressed by how his life-passion has continued for over 60 years. He is a thinker, a novelist and a good friend. I am happy to have the pleasure to have known him all my life. Most great artists don't get appreciated until they pass. I think he'll be noticed in the years to come. Additionally, my old friend, you are right about one thing for sure: *The world is pretty screwed-up these days.*

- Leonard P. Vaglia

Thank you for your persistence in writing your books, your drive to write is truly amazing. I was just reading your book entitled: 'Artificial Intelligense' and liked the many twists the A.I. Android made to the history of the world I grew up in. The chapter of 'Doug Jurci' especially touched a chord with me and really reminds me of my childhood. I loved the ending which makes you think about the fallacies that are in A.I.

- Dominic Backowski

"They" should have given us REAL INTELLIGENCE, not a fake one.

- TSC.

TS Caladan

Doug was born the only son of Rose and Steve Yurchey in Bridgeville, PA. in 1951. A loner, he drew pictures and dreamed of big/bright fantasy-worlds that were inside the comic book adventures he cherished. Movies, TV, stories, art, thrilled the young man, especially sci-fi and anything that had to do with aliens and life on other planets. He grew up interested in sports and earned a half-scholarship in tennis to Edinboro. After college, his interests turned to astronomy and various mysteries.

An unexpected event occurred: In 1973, he fell in love with a psychic who channeled. A 4-year marriage and a 'virtual Close Encounter' later, the young man was motivated to discover the truth in everything<. Odd occurrences happened during a strange marriage where spoons and keys bent with the powers of the mind. They met mentalist Uri Geller at this time. Wife Katrina did similar telepathic feats and their closest friends witnessed extraordinary things. In 1977, the marriage ended.

Doug moved to LA in 1982. He worked on the Simpsons Show in 1990-1991 as a background "Clean-Up" artist. After 2000, he became a prolific writer with many online articles, radio interviews and YouTubes of his work on Atlantis, Nikola Tesla and the World Grid. He was on 'Coast-to-Coast with George Noory' radio show and gave "the best interview since John Lear." Doug was filmed by National Geographic filmmaker Diego D'Innocenzo because of his theories on the ancient, rust-less, Iron Pillar in New Delhi. Nine million Italians saw the production on a TV Science show called 'Voyager,' with special-effects. His writing dreams came true and he was published by TWB Press in 2015. Now *TS Caladan,* the author's interests are Modern Mysteries and conspiracies or secrets behind Hollywood and the Illuminati. Then he discovered the Mandela Effect in 2019, which *changed everything~.* Tray Caladan is a mystery himself. He has spent more than 50 years of pure, honest, scientific research and today uses artwork and wild/far-out, sci-fi stories to deliver his conclusions and positive messages...*and, still, no one believes him.* [A few do].

Contact information for Tray Samuel Caladan:

tscaladan@gmail.com

Questions and comments are very welcome. Readers will receive quick replies. Thank you very much.

~tsc

Books written by TS Caladan (DH Jetson):

1) The Continuum

2) Son of Zog

3) The Cydonian War

4), 5) Science-Faction [Vol. 1 & 2], short stories

6) ANAGRAMACRON

7) inspiration

8) 2099, Transia~

9) The New Men and the New World

10) Beyond Barronsland

11) Mandela Effect

12) Best of TS Caladan

13) Mandela Effect II

14) Collected Comedy of TS Caladan

15) TS Caladan's Comedy II

16) Pez Wars

17) The PEZ-Effect

18) Ceana

19) PEZ 4 Ever

20) My Cat Book

21) Artificial *Intelligense*

22) Teran Tales

https://www.twbpress.com

Science Fiction – Supernatural – Horror – Thriller

and more